CHOCOLATE
SECRETS

Other books by Zelda Benjamin:

Brooklyn Ballerina

CHOCOLATE SECRETS

•

Zelda Benjamin

AVALON BOOKS
NEW YORK

Published by Thomas Bouregy & Co., Inc.
160 Madison Avenue, New York, NY 10016

Library of Congress Cataloging-in-Publication Data

Benjamin, Zelda.
 Chocolate secrets / Zelda Benjamin.
      p.   cm.
 ISBN-13: 978-0-8034-9884-6 (acid-free paper)
 I. Title.
 PS3602.E664C47   2008
 813'.6—dc22   2007037555

PRINTED IN THE UNITED STATES OF AMERICA
ON ACID-FREE PAPER
BY HADDON CRAFTSMEN, BLOOMSBURG, PENNSYLVANIA

Chapter One

Sunday horoscope: Beware of new responsibilities.

To blame the planets for a sudden change in her plans would be like blaming the thermometer for the sudden dip in the temperature. The Indian summer Alex Martinelli longed for had been short-lived. Seated in the front seat of her grandfather's delivery van, she inched her collar up to ward off the chill. The decadent smell of Grandpa Max's chocolate truffles permeated the chilly air. Turning up the heat could melt his precious candy.

She stifled a yawn. Her grandfather had been reluctant to accept her offer to assist him with his booth at the Atlantic Avenue fair. Alex had just walked in from the night shift at County Hospital where she worked as an ER nurse when Chloe, Max's talented young chocolate

1

chef, called to tell him she was too sick to join him at the fair.

Grandpa Max and Chloe had planned to preview their secret truffle recipe today. If Max even suspected Alex had lied about not being tired, he would insist she forget about helping him and get right into bed. For a brief moment the thought of resting beneath her snug comforter left her with a passing feeling of warmth.

She lowered the visor to protect her eyes from the rising sun and picked up the newspaper. Grandpa Max had been reading the sports section as he waited for Alex to change out of her scrubs. Systematically folding the paper to page twenty-six, she proceeded to read her daily horoscope. Maybe something good would happen to compensate for her feeling of sleep deprivation.

New responsibilities could bring on more work or put you in a situation you are not willing to venture into. In spite of the truth in those words she couldn't leave her grandfather alone at the fair.

She tossed the Sunday paper back on the seat, picked up her cell phone, and dialed Chloe's number.

On the other end of the line Chloe's usual spunky greeting was replaced with a hoarse whisper, reinforcing Alex's offer to stand in for the sick chocolate chef. Alex could only imagine how disappointed Chloe must be to miss the fair.

Chloe wasn't the only one with the flu. It seemed like every nurse on the night shift in the ER at County had called out with similar symptoms which is how Alex, who usually worked the day shift, ended up on the grave-yard shift.

It didn't take long to drive the few short blocks to the fair. The flow of traffic on this bustling Brooklyn thoroughfare had been detoured so the vendors could make full use of the wide street. Max turned onto a cross avenue and parked the van.

Standing alongside the pink van with chocolate brown letters, Alex watched her grandfather unload his delicious cargo. One by one the booths around them began to come alive. The vendors shouldered bags, boxes, and crates filled with colorful fall vegetables, crafts, and household goods. Like busy little ants they unloaded and arranged their wares for display. Even Madame Nilda, the neighborhood astrologer, was there. Dressed in her flowing silks and beads, she looked very different from the sweet old lady who came into Grandpa's shop for her daily chocolate fix, a delicate dark chocolate with hazelnut paste.

On the other side of the street a group of firefighters and paramedics from the local firehouse were setting up a booth. By the look of the guys carrying the boxes, she assumed they were peddling those hunky firefighter calendars. Maybe she'd stop by and get one for Chloe or her friend Sarah. Sarah and Chloe, unlike Alex, had a thing for those sexy heroes.

One of the guys looked back and smiled. With dark hair and sparkling blue eyes that she could see from across the narrow street, she was sure he had a page on the calendar. What month would he be? A Leo, perhaps, a natural performer, loves children, and has love affairs. As pleasant as it was to watch his biceps bulge beneath his navy FDNY T-shirt, her practical side surfaced. She was here to work, not to enjoy the scenery. With a shake of her head she banished her silly thoughts and walked around the van to find her grandfather.

"We've got a good location. Those fire rescue people will draw a big crowd." He carried a tray filled with his chocolate truffles. There was a mischievous twinkle in his eyes that had nothing to do with the decadence of his product. "Good-looking bunch of men across the street. I'd bet some of them would be interested in a pretty girl like you."

Alex had been there and done that. Her two older brothers and her father were firefighters. After her divorce they were always trying to fix her up with someone from the department. She had enough men in her life who ran into burning buildings every day. She refused to date any of their friends and wanted nothing to do with their matchmaking.

"Grandpa, you know I'm not interested in dating a fireman."

"Sure, sure. I heard it all before. You gotta start dating again. You can't have babies on your own. In my time a girl your age, thirty-five, should have had a couple of kids already." Grandpa Max narrowed his eyes. "Look what happened with your ex-husband. Thought you knew that one. Didn't you?"

"Josh and I did know each other, Grandpa." She

released a long, tired sigh. "We just didn't agree on some things."

"Like having babies," Grandpa mumbled and walked away. To a stranger, his comments would sound cruel but to Alex they just reflected the difference in their generations. She picked up a pile of pink bags with CHOCOLATE BOUTIQUE written in deep brown in each corner and followed her grandfather.

The Atlantic Avenue Fair was an important fall event for all the vendors in this busy Brooklyn business district. It was especially important to Grandpa Max and Chloe.

The production of their delicious candies had been shrouded in secrecy. It didn't bother Alex that even she wasn't privy to the recipe. Making chocolate was much too precise for her. She preferred the magical effect of the finished product.

Alex didn't plan on hanging around all day. She'd help Grandpa set up his candy-making apparatus, then leave. But as she watched the sidewalks and streets fill with vendors and shoppers, babies in strollers and dogs on leashes, shoppers and schmoozers, she found herself caught up in the excitement and no longer felt tired. What a wonderful opportunity for Grandpa Max and Chloe to introduce their explosive epitome of chocolate delight.

Autumn was the perfect time for street fairs. The trees were at the height of fall foliage. She watched an industrious squirrel scamper through a small iron gate and dig at the base of a maple tree. A gentle breeze rustled through the leaves. The smell of fresh baked cakes drifted from the direction of the firefighters' booth.

So, they're peddling more than just those sexy calendars, Alex thought. Could be competition for her grandfather. She'd have to go over and take a look.

There was no doubt her grandfather smelled the sweet baked goods too. "Why don't you go check them out." He nudged her away from his booth.

She hesitated.

"C'mon, you don't have to marry one of them. Just buy a cake. I've gotta know if they're going to steal my business."

"Are you sure you don't want me to watch the temperature on the sugar?" Alex looked at Grandpa's special cauldron filled with cane sugar. As part of his display, Max planned to demonstrate how he pulled melted sugar into candy canes.

She watched his short, stocky body lean over the pot designed specially for use away from his shop. It was smaller than the one he used every day. She hoped he remembered to adjust the recipe to fit the size of the pot. Concerned for his safety, she watched as her grandfather's fingers, still strong and straight from decades of mixing sticky concoctions, stirred the gooey substance that would eventually become beautiful candy ribbons.

"Check out the other vendors and get yourself something to eat. It was nice enough you offered to help me set up."

"Can you manage?" Alex hesitated before walking away.

"I'll be fine."

She gave her grandfather a skeptical look. The other day Chloe had told her how Grandpa Max appeared a little forgetful, forgetting to add the stripes to his peppermint candies or the sticks to his lollipops. Ever since her grandmother had passed away, Grandpa Max had insisted on continuing to work, never missing a day in his shop.

"You're the tired, overworked one." Grandpa's droopy eyes wrinkled with concern.

Alex knew her grandfather was right. Not only did she pick up extra shifts in the ER, she tried to help him in his candy shop on her days off. At five feet, one hundred and ten pounds there wasn't much of her to spread around.

"Go. I've got work to do." He nudged her gently.

In front of the fire rescue booth a crowd of mostly parents with children lined up along the curb. The firehouse had parked a ladder truck and hose engine on the corner. She stretched on her tiptoes to see what everyone was watching. The minute she spotted the dark-haired firefighter, the one she glimpsed earlier, she understood why the crowd had gathered. In one hand he effortlessly balanced a tool that resembled a medieval instrument of torture.

His voice, strong and impressive, projected an energy and power that attracted looks from the men as well as the women. Up close he was even more stunning than he had been from a distance.

"This is a Halligan." He pointed to an evil-looking

metal thingamajig balanced on the end of a long stick. "It's used for poking into walls and ceilings so the crew can hunt down any embers that can reignite."

Alex forced herself to tear her gaze from his strong, rugged profile. The best way around the crowd led her directly in front of his booth. She stopped for a moment and watched as a little boy tugged on the bunker pants of the strikingly handsome firefighter. He tousled the kid's hair. His gesture was so genuine. She smiled.

He must have mistaken her smile for a greeting. He laid the halligan down and stepped behind the booth. With a wave of his hand he offered her a glimpse of their display. She saw not only calendars but some less-than-perfect chocolate cakes as well.

"Care to try a slice? The money goes to a worthy cause—the burn unit at County." His smile was as decadent as the chocolate oozing over the side of the not-so-perfect looking cake.

Alex could feel the color heating her cheeks as she looked up. Putting aside her feelings, she reached into her pocketbook. "How much for the whole cake?" She had worked at the burn unit before transferring to the ER and knew the money from these cakes would be put to good use.

The firefighter ran his hand across the top of his military haircut. "Wow. You want the whole cake." A boyish charm sparkled in his blue eyes. "Don't you want to try a slice first?"

"No thanks, not today. I'm working at the candy booth and my horoscope advised against indulging in too many sweets." She looked up at him and asked again, "How much?"

Ignoring her question he stepped around the counter. "So your horoscope said to avoid sweets?" With a raised brow he studied her. "Do you always do what your horoscope suggests?"

"It's just a guideline." Alex wasn't disturbed by his reaction. Most people reacted with surprise when she talked about her charts and sun sign. Anxious to get back to her grandfather she pointed to a cake. "What do you think the baker will consider for the entire cake?"

"I never really thought about selling the entire cake to one customer." He hooked his fingers in the nook of his suspenders. "I baked these cakes myself."

"Really?" She stared at him, amazed.

"Honest." He made a little *X* over his heart.

Alex took notice of the name under his imaginary *X*. "Well, Mike . . ."—she leaned closer for a better look at the last name blocked by his finger—"Simone." She stifled a gasp. Simone's weren't suppose to look like this gorgeous man.

"Is something wrong?" He reached out to steady her.

Remembering all her childhood perceptions of anyone belonging to the Simone family, she stepped out of his grasp. A long time ago a terrible man named Sal Simone had stolen something sacred from her grandfather. Year after year her grandfather warned the next generation to stay clear of those thieving Simones. Her childhood imagination created a picture of fire breathing, Medusa-like monsters.

It was true she had never met a Simone and thought they all must have died off. But this man was very much alive. Definitely surrounded by fire, he bore no resemblance to a gross monster. The only thing she could imagine this Simone stealing would be a few hearts. How would Grandpa Max react if he realized the handsome man who had caught his granddaughter's eye was a Simone?

Fumbling with her wallet she pulled out a twenty. "Here, keep the change. It's for a worthy cause." Pinched between her thumb and finger the bill, flapped in the breeze. "And keep the cake. You can resell it or whatever."

"That's really generous, but I can't keep the cake and your money." He didn't seem to notice her uneasiness.

"I insist." She placed the bill on the counter and turned to leave.

He was relentless. "I noticed you're working across the street. I'll stop by later with your change."

He had noticed her. Alex's thoughts suddenly became suspicious. Why would this hunk of a man—a Simone—who had every woman on the street vying for his attention be looking at her?

"That won't be necessary," she chided.

"Sure it is. Maybe we can compare chocolate recipes."

"Oh no." Alex looked up at his sparkling blue eyes and lost her thought process. Stumbling for the right words she finally said, "I don't actually make the candy. I'm only helping out today." Even if it was a coincidence that this gorgeous man's name was Simone, Alex couldn't chance upsetting her grandfather.

A little blond girl with a small boy in tow tugged on Simone's leg. "Hey, Mr. Fireman, can we go on your truck?"

Before he effortlessly hoisted the kids onto the engine, Simone turned to Alex and said, "I'll catch you later."

Grateful for the distraction, Alex managed a mumbled, "Yeah, later." She turned and walked away.

When she was a safe distance away, she couldn't resist glancing over her shoulder. Simone muscle's flexed as he demonstrated to the kids how to fold a firehose. She could easily become distracted watching this man play with the neighborhood children. She forced herself to turn away.

Alex wasn't the only one watching with interest. She noticed Madame Nilda had left her stand.

"Good morning, Alex." The older woman met Alex's gaze. "Want me to read the cards and see if one of those handsome young men is in your future?"

"No thanks. No fire rescue men for me." Did she think Alex was flirting with this guy? Nilda, like everyone in this close-knit neighborhood, knew that after her father's emphysema had forced him to retire from the fire department, Alex vowed never to date men who ran into burning buildings. Especially men named Simone.

However, her forced indifference could not kill her curiosity about Mike Simone. Alex had a feeling an old timer like Nilda would have some information about the feud between the Simones and Martinellis.

Trying to sound casual she asked, "I noticed his last name is Simone. You wouldn't happen to know what my grandfather has against them?"

"Things like that are between families. You'll have to ask Max." A customer approached Nilda's booth. She seemed relieved to be called away from this conversation.

"He seems nice enough." Alex said to the fortune-teller's back but got no response. She wondered what cosmic influences challenged a man like that? A hero. A protector. He liked kids. He might be a Taurus or a Leo. Leo was a fixed fire sign. She was a Scorpio, a fixed water sign—definitely not compatible with a Leo.

Turning her attention away from Nilda and the fire-fighters she proceeded in the opposite direction. She stopped to buy a cup of coffee and a Danish before she headed back in the direction of her grandfather's booth.

Alex hadn't gotten very far when someone shouted, "Something's on fire!"

"A fire," she repeated in a choked voice.

She glanced at the fire rescue booth. Were they simulating a fire to demonstrate their work? No. The flames shooting into the air were nowhere near the fire truck. They seemed to be coming from the middle of the block, much too close to the spot where Grandpa Max had his candy booth. Where there was fire there could very well be an old man making candy.

"Call 911!" the coffee vendor shouted.

Her instincts as an ER nurse took over. She handed her coffee to the stranger standing next to her. Ignoring the hysterical cries from the spectators, she charged back through the crowd. The closer she got, the smoke grew thicker.

"It's Grandpa's cauldron." Alex felt her heart skip a beat and picked up her pace. In front of her grandfather's booth, she ran right into the solid body of a man in blue. She looked up and found herself gazing at the handsome face of the cake baker. Over his shoulder she saw black clouds of smoke shooting up toward the cloudless sky.

"Stand back." He grabbed her arm and tried to stop her from getting closer to the flaming cauldron.

Another firefighter found his way through the maze of boxes and crates behind the confection stand. He reached for the heavy lid grandpa kept next to the pot. There was a loud clank as the cover smothered the flames. And a muffled "ouch" from Grandpa, who tried to douse a small fire started by a renegade clump of sugar.

"I'm a nurse." Surprised by the gentleness of Simone's grip she pried his fingers from her arm. "And that foolish old man trying to put out the fire is my grandfather.

He looked at Alex and then her grandfather. An understanding look crossed his face and he let her pass. This couldn't be happening. There had been no hint of a disaster in her horoscope, only a warning not to get carried away by good deeds. She looked back at the firefighter trying to control the curious crowd. There had definitely been no mention of an intervention from a dark-haired stranger.

While Alex's mind worked in one direction, her body moved with an efficiency that came from her combined experiences as a nurse in both a burn unit and a municipal ER. She recognized the smell of burnt flesh and focused immediately on the burns on her grandfather's hand. There was no time to ask for the details that led up to the accident. Automatically she reached for the nearest items that could be used to dress the wound, a clean cheesecloth and cold water.

"Here. Use these instead." Simone had assigned the task of crowd control to a passing police officer. He stood beside her with a red tackle box filled with emergency supplies.

Alex reached for the bottle of saline and sterile bandage he offered. "Thanks." She looked up and immediately saw the compassion in his face. Hoping to ease her own anxiety, she smiled and said, "I should have followed my horoscope and stayed in bed this morning."

"I'm glad you didn't." The tilt that tipped the corner of his mouth when he smiled made her pulse race. "And so is your patient," he added.

Alex turned her attention back to her grandfather who was not a willing participant. "Sit still," she ordered.

The acrid smell of smoke and crisp, burnt sugar filled the air. Paramedics on standby in case of a medical emergency arrived. They helped Simone's partner douse the pot with foam from a fire extinguisher.

White foam covered everything, even the pretty pink bags.

"My pot, my precious pot. Look what they're doing to my copper cauldron."

"We'll get you another pot." Alex looked at her grandfather's hand. Bright red skin with small water-filled blisters contracted the skin. "Your burn needs to be taken care of." She poured the saline over his hand.

With most of her attention centered on cleaning her grandfather's wound, Alex still managed to watch the fireman.

Grandpa Max studied him too. "You married, young man?"

"No sir. Still looking for the right girl."

Alex cringed when her grandfather leaned forward and squinted for a better look at the name on the shirt. FDNY was written in bold red on the left side of Mike's navy blue sweatshirt. She locked her hand around her grandfather's wrist, hoping to distract him from reading the lighter stitches under the emblem.

"Simone. That's your name?" With his good hand, Grandpa Max reached up. He poked the dark-haired firefighter in the chest.

"Yes, sir, Mike Simone."

"Have any family in the neighborhood?" Max, forgetting for a minute that he had badly burned his hand, spit over his shoulder in a gesture to ward off evil spirits. Without giving Simone a chance to answer he mumbled, "Never met a good Simone."

"Grandpa, hold still."

Ignoring Alex, Max continued grumbling at Mike. "I bet you're a descendant of those thieves. You've got the same plundering eyes as that thief, Sal Simone."

"Grandpa!"

"I'm not having any Simone offer me help. Hmm, you would be the one to show up when my precious candy is going up in smoke."

She could feel the color heat her cheeks as she busied herself with her task. With her eyes still on the handsome fireman, she wrapped the bandage over the wet gauze.

A puzzled look knitted Simone's brow, but otherwise he seemed unaffected by Max's accusation. He turned to Alex and handed her a roll of paper tape." You might want to secure the end of that gauze."

"Thanks for the suggestion," she retorted, unsure why she was suddenly cautious of him. "I've done this a few times." She tore off a piece of tape and fastened the ends of the dressing.

"Don't tell her what to do. She's an ER nurse. She knows her stuff," Max snapped. "And don't get any ideas about her either."

Alex wasn't sure which was worse: her grandfather's attempt at matchmaking or his rudeness.

"She did a good job," Mike said, unruffled by Max's comments.

Grandpa Max made a face. "You got an Uncle Sal?" he asked.

"Yes, sir. I have a great uncle on my grandfather's side. His name is Sal Simone."

"I knew it!" Max looked up at Alex. "Why'd you bring him over here?"

"Grandpa, I didn't bring him. You're lucky he was close by." She looked around at the smoky mess, and sighed. "It could have been worse," she added in Mike's defense and to neutralize her grandfather's growing hostility.

"Well, he's here now, and I don't want his help. There's bad blood in those Simones."

Alex sensed the rage building in this usually calm old man. "Grandpa, I don't know what Mike's uncle did to you, but you need to calm down."

"Sal." Max's face turned red and he choked out the rest of his words. "Like a thief in the night he stole my secret chocolate recipe." To emphasize his point he snapped his good fingers in Mike's direction. "Just like that, your uncle had me fooled." He shook his head and added, "Even worse, I thought he was my friend."

Alex felt her grandfather's pain. Loyalty and friendship meant a lot to him. She tried to imagine how difficult it must be for him to talk about this now, sitting here with his bandaged hand and Chloe's sensational chocolates burnt to a crisp.

She looked at Mike who had tactfully taken a few steps back. He turned away and appeared to be surveying the damage. It was a smart move on his part. Anything he could say would only further upset her grandfather.

Mike's partner, Danny joined the group. He lifted Max's hand and asked, "Did you see the burn, Simone?"

Mike turned his attention back to Alex and Max. "Second and third degree across the palm and his fingers."

"Is that bad?" Max glared at Mike and looked at Alex for confirmation.

"Yes, Grandpa. Third degree is very bad," Alex tried to encourage her grandfather to stand.

"Let's get you into the ambulance." Mike and his partner were more persuasive and helped Max to his feet.

"Ambulance?" Grandpa Max pulled away from Mike. "What ambulance? I'm not going to any hospital. I have important work to do here." Grandpa winced when he waved his bandaged hand in the air. "You said so yourself, she did a good job. No need for me to get in that darn ambulance. I'm going to clean up the mess you guys made of my equipment and sell some more candy."

"Grandpa," Alex's tone was firm. "You need to go to the hospital and have the burns properly cleaned and cared for."

Alex knew how important the exposure at today's fair was for her grandfather and Chloe. They had spent days blending the delicate chocolate centers of Max's signature truffles with an array of spices handpicked by Chloe. By offering samples to the crowd at the fair, they had hoped to create interest and expand the market for their chocolate treasures. With Chloe home sick and Grandpa on the way to the hospital, that idea had just gone up in smoke.

This was not the time to try and think of an alternative

plan to introduce Grandpa's velvety truffles. The paramedics team had just rolled their stretcher behind the booth.

"What happened to Martinelli?" a young, clean-shaven paramedic asked.

Max Martinelli had been making his sweet confections at the same location for over fifty years. With a son retired from the department, Max donated generously to fire rescue charities. Most of the fire rescue people in the area knew him well.

"Is that baby-faced Ralphie?" Max asked.

"How you doing, Mr. Martinelli?" Ralphie's soft, round chin wrinkled with concern when he looked at Max's bandaged hand. "You giving these people a hard time?"

"He doesn't want to go to the hospital," Mike's partner said, then gave Alex an exaggerated wink.

"I'm not going any place with a rookie paramedic who's not even old enough to shave." Max planted his feet on the ground and refused to budge. "And I'm definitely not getting into an ambulance with anyone named Simone!"

The paramedics did not have all day to stand around and wait for her grandfather to agree to go to the hospital. She needed to convince him that getting in the ambulance was vital to saving the use of his hand.

She reached for his unbandaged hand. While holding it gently, she explained, "If you don't get the proper attention, you'll never be able to make those wonderful truffles."

"She knows what she's talking about," Mike's partner said.

"But I'm not staying in that place overnight."

"We'll see when you get there." Alex released a sigh of relief. She watched as her grandfather reluctantly allowed the paramedics to help him onto the stretcher. He suddenly seemed so frail as he leaned into the strong muscular arms supporting him.

"She riding with us?" the ambulance driver asked.

"Of course she is. You think I'm putting myself in the care of a bunch of rookies?" Grandpa looked at Ralphie.

The crowd made a narrow path so the rescuers could wheel Max's stretcher to the ambulance. Flanked by the paramedics, he looked like a king with his bearers.

Alex followed. Mike walked beside her. He nodded in her grandfather's direction. "He's going to need to see a hand specialist. You might want to call someone you know. Have them meet you at County."

With so much happening, Alex was surprised she hadn't thought to make the call. "I do have someone I can call."

Mike was smart to keep his distance from the agitated old man. At the ambulance he reached out to open the doors with ease. Alex couldn't help but notice how the fabric of his shirt stretched over his rolled-up sleeves. She tried to get a closer look at his emblem, to see if he worked an engine or a ladder company. Her father and brothers often told friendly jokes about the engine men being shorter, to help keep them below the level of the smoke. When he stood close she didn't have to strain her neck to look up at him. She guessed he was about five feet nine. Dismissing her thoughts with a shrug, she concluded he was probably on an engine team.

There were more important issues to think about. She took out her cell phone but hesitated. Should she call her ex-husband, Josh, a plastic surgeon? He had been on call at the ER last night and told her he had scheduled some Sunday morning follow-ups. She assumed he would be in his office but was surprised when his answering service picked up.

Alex left her name. "No message," she said, then proceeded to dial his cell number.

The phone rang several times before Josh picked up. "Alex, I thought you'd still be in bed, catching up on your sleep. Why are you calling?"

"My grandfather had an accident. He's going to need a hand specialist." Alex held her breath and waited for Josh to answer. She smiled at Mike pretending the silence on the other end didn't exist.

"I can't, Alex. I'm tied up all day."

Alex thought she heard a female voice. "Are you with someone?" she asked.

As usual Josh had an explanation. "One of the drug reps invited me to brunch."

"On a Sunday?" Alex turned her back to Mike. She cupped her hand over the phone and whispered so no one would hear her disappointment. "Can't you reschedule?"

"She's got a very busy agenda. We'd really like to get hold of this product as soon as possible."

All Alex's old feelings, insecurities and doubts during their five-year marriage suddenly surfaced. He didn't even have the decency to ask what had happened to Max.

"See what you can do. I'll talk to you later." Her last words caught in her throat. They were a lie. They had been divorced for over a year. Alex tried to keep their relationship friendly because of their professional association, but it was getting more and more difficult. He was no longer the neighborhood boy she had married. A pompous, self-important attitude had surfaced with his success. At the moment she never wanted to speak to Josh again.

How could he refuse to meet them in the ER? This was her grandfather who needed his expertise, not some stranger who found his name in an insurance book.

Alex pressed the OFF button with a little too much energy. Her phone slipped out of her hand.

Mike Simone stood close by. He reached out and caught her phone before it hit the ground. "Everything okay?" he asked.

"No problem. He'll try to get there." She chewed on her lower lip and stole a glance at him. He regarded her with a narrowed look that hinted he suspected there was a problem.

Alex waited while the paramedics got her grandfather settled in the ambulance.

Mike stood across from her. He watched the medics load up the ambulance. He didn't appear to be anything like Josh. How could he be? He liked kids and he risked his life to save other people. That was what fire-fighters did.

She reminded herself not only of her grandfather's hostility toward him, but her vow never to get involved with a firefighter. A vow made after her father had been diagnosed with emphysema. A vow that now, looking at this kind, strong man, who happened to be a Simone, seemed ridiculous.

However, she was curious about one thing. Just before she stepped into the ambulance she turned to Mike. As casually as she could manage, she asked, "What's your sign?"

"My sign?" He gave her a sidelong glance that signaled he had been taken completely by surprise.

"Your horoscope."

The beginning of a smile curved the corners of his lips. "I'm an asparagus," he answered.

Chapter Two

Horoscope: Face those relationship
issues you've swept under the rug.

Alex sighed as the ambulance rolled to a stop on the ramp outside the county hospital ER. She didn't want to be back here so soon, not on her day off. She glanced at her grandfather. His eyes were shut. A whiff of nitrous oxide to ease his pain had done its job.

"We're here." Ralphie swung open the rear ambulance door. With help from the other paramedic, he lifted the stretcher onto the ground.

Inside the ER they were greeted by Cyndi, one of the senior nurses. "Whatcha got?" she asked the ambulance crew while she visually assessed Max's bandaged hand. "There are no empty beds. Can he walk to triage?" Then she looked up and noticed Alex. "What

24

are you doing here?" She asked. She smiled and added, "This is your grandpa?"

Alex looked around the crowded emergency room. "Yes. This is my grandfather, Max. He's got a pretty significant burn to his right hand."

"Hi, Mr. Martinelli. Do you recognize me? I'm the girl who buys a pound of your chocolate-covered fruit every Friday." Cyndi's calm hazel eyes focused only on Max, avoiding the chaos around her. You could tell she saw beyond his poker-faced facade.

"We'll start you on a hall stretcher and get you taken care of real soon." She squeezed his uninjured hand.

Alex hated seeing him so vulnerable. "Grandpa, if you're in pain you have to tell us." She knew part of his expression was due to his dislike of doctors and hospitals.

"Just get me out of here, and I'll be fine."

"Let's get him signed in, and I'll get an order for pain meds," Cyndi said.

While her grandfather was moved to an ER bed, Alex helped expedite the triage procedure. She answered the usual questions regarding his insurance, allergies, and past medical condition.

Grandpa Max sank back against his pillow and closed his eyes. With his uninjured hand, he clung to the bedrail while the ER physician started to unwrap Alex's makeshift bandage. "Where's that nurse with my medication?" His heavy gray eyebrows drew together.

Alex placed her hand over her grandfather's. "It's coming, Grandpa."

"We'll wait for his pain medication before I continue." The doctor looked up at Alex and asked, "He might need a plastic surgeon, a hand specialist. Did you call . . ."

"Josh." Alex knew the ER staff often felt awkward about her divorce. "He can't come."

"No problem. Plastics on-call is already here. If you don't mind waiting, he's busy with a complicated dog bite at the moment." He turned to Max and said, "We'll make you comfortable while you're waiting."

Cyndi arrived with equipment for an IV.

"What's that for?" Max was suddenly attentive.

"I'm going to start an IV and give you some morphine for the pain."

Max gave her a cautious look. "You leaving that thing in me? I'll be able to go home, won't I?"

"Grandpa, let her do her job," Alex said.

Once the medication took effect, Max relaxed and the doctor was able to pull off the rest of the dressing.

Max looked up at Cyndi and said, "You girls do good work here. I'm going to see that you get a supply of your favorite chocolate."

Alex knew her grandfather would be true to his words. His offer to Cyndi gave Alex an idea. She'd stop at the chocolate shop after they were through here and put together a box of Chloe's best chocolates to bring to the firehouse. After all, even if his name was Simone, Mike had come to the rescue. She wondered what kind of chocolate he would like, dark or light. Would he prefer Chloe's hot spicy centers or a sweet delicate blend?

"Can't talk you into working, can I?" Cyndi asked, bringing her back to the present. "You could throw on a pair of scrubs and help out?"

Alex looked around. It wasn't even noon and the staff had a look she recognized. The waiting room was crowded and the ambulances kept coming. Her grandfather looked comfortable.

She had to be here anyway. "Get me a pair of scrubs."

The day at the fair had taken an unusual twist and turn. Mike was glad to be back at the firehouse with the familiar smell of diesel fuel. He jumped from the truck and directed Danny as he backed the engine into the garage. Surrounded by oversized tools and smoky bunker gear he felt at home.

Danny hosed the engine, and Mike picked up a clean rag to dry the remaining water spots. While performing the mindless task, his thoughts drifted. He thought about what Max Martinelli had said about the Simone family.

Mike had always been compared to his Uncle Sal, an eccentric old man who lived on a sailboat in Bimini. They said he inherited his talent for making chocolate concoctions from his strange uncle.

The truth was Mike enjoyed baking. A logical thinker, he liked the precision of the preparation, measuring and mixing in exact amounts and producing a perfect cake. Well, almost perfect. Getting the shape of the cake even was the least of his problems. If he could find the missing ingredient in his chocolate frosting, there was a good chance he could win the firefighters bake-off.

The coveted trophy would be displayed at the firehouse, but his prize money would be donated to the burn center at County Hospital. However, winning first prize did not seem likely. His cake might be a little off-center but it was moist and tasty. The problem was with his frosting. What good was a chocolate cake if it had bad frosting? He had tried over and over to find the perfect blend between the cake and the topping. There had to be someone who could help him find the missing ingredient. Someone with a lot of experience in blending chocolate, someone like the old man at the candy booth.

He turned to Danny and asked, "What do you know about Old Man Martinelli?"

"He's been around the neighborhood a long time. Why ya asking?"

"He seemed to know something about my family. I've never heard my parents speak about any Martinellis." Mike watched Danny clean a stray water spot off the side of the engine.

Danny was a real senior. He'd been with the department over twenty years. He had looked out for Mike when he was a rookie, showing him how to use the gear and tools. And Danny knew the streets and people of this area better than anyone at the firehouse. Not only Mike, but all the new guys had a lot of respect for Danny.

"The old man's son was a captain with the 206. Went out on benefits a few years ago. I hear he's doing good now that he's retired. Could be related to something that happened when his son was still with the department." Danny tossed his rag into a bucket. "He's also got two grandsons with the department. One's with a ladder company in the Bronx, and the other's stationed in the city."

"It's nothing to do with the department. He said my great uncle stole a recipe from him."

"A recipe." Danny laughed. "Go figure. Some of the people in this neighborhood have been here for so long they all have a story to tell." He slapped Mike on the shoulder and said, "Forget about the old man. Come on, let's get a cup of coffee and some of your almost-perfect cake."

Upstairs in the kitchen, Danny poured two cups of black firehouse coffee and cut himself a slice of cake. He took his mug and cake over to the table and unfolded the Sunday paper.

Mike watched Danny take a huge forkful of his less-than-perfect confection. "You guys will eat anything." He shrugged and turned away.

The paramedic team that responded to the fire at the fair was back.

Ralphie strutted over to Mike and slapped him on the

back. "Hey, Simone, Old Man Martinelli was lucky you were close by."

"Just doing my job." Mike took a sip of his coffee.

"That's not what his granddaughter said on the ride over to County."

"What did she say?" Mike looked nonchalantly over the rim of his cup.

"Said you were a nice guy."

"Like I said, just doing my job." Mike had hoped she would remember him a little differently. It was okay to be a nice guy but he thought he had seen a glimmer of interest when she looked at him. Maybe he had been mistaken, or maybe she believed those things her grandfather said about his family. "How did the old man do?"

"He started to feel some pain so we gave him a whiff of the nitrous. He's something else, that Max."

"And the granddaughter ain't so bad either," the other paramedic said.

"I've worked with Alex at County. She's a good nurse," Ralphie said.

The medics comment about Alex sparked Mike's interest. "You work at County?"

"I pick up some shifts in the ER on my days off. You interested?"

"In some extra shifts?" The department required all firefighters to be paramedics too, but Mike wasn't interested in working in the ER. He shook his head. "No thanks."

"I get it. You're interested in the granddaughter. Gotta

warn ya. Don't waste your time with her," Ralphie said.

"Why not?" Mike asked.

"She won't date firefighters," Ralphie stated as if her social preference was common knowledge.

"How do you know? Did you ask her out?" Mike rubbed his fingers across the scruff on his cheek.

"What if I did?"

"You're not a firefighter." Mike gave the baby-faced paramedic a playful shove. "And you don't even shave. Maybe she likes grown-up men."

"Nope. She won't date anyone who works for the department," Ralphie said.

"And don't forget the old man doesn't like anyone named Simone." Danny peered over the top of the Sunday comics.

"That doesn't seem like a good reason." Mike grew serious. "Maybe she just hasn't met the right firefighter. You would think anyone with family in the department knows we're the best."

"She's a nurse," Danny said. "She knows how many hours we spend in the ER getting stitched up, X-rayed and having our burns treated." Danny seemed to be full of suggestions. "Who knows; maybe she just doesn't date."

"Of course she does." Ralphie jumped to her defense. "She's just getting over a divorce."

"Any kids?" Mike asked.

"No," Ralphie answered. "There was gossip that no kids was a reason for the divorce."

Mike wanted to ask more questions, but this was not the time or the place. Diving into Alex's private life in front of the other guys would be in poor taste. "I bet he's a plastic surgeon," he said then added, "a hand specialist."

"How'd ya guess?"

"She called him when her grandfather got injured."

"Jerk. Probably said he couldn't meet them in the ER." Ralphie seemed to know what he was talking about. A rookie paramedic with a big heart, he always asked the guys about their families. Mike would bet he did the same at the hospital.

"So what do you think I should do?" Mike put his arm around Ralphie's shoulder.

"You could read her horoscope. She's always checking the paper for her forecast."

"The idea is not very logical but it might be a place to start." Mike recalled her interest in his sign and some casual comments she had made. He hadn't taken her seriously. Afterall, an analytical thinker like himself would never pay attention to such an irrational process.

Danny suddenly showed interest in their conversation. "You guys might not be as stupid as you look." He jumped up and waved the magazine section of the paper between Mike and Ralphie. "Here it is, boys. If the little lady really believes all that mumbo jumbo, this could be your lucky day. Right here in this article could be the help you need."

Ralphie grabbed the paper and read the headlines out loud. "Fame, fortune, and a good time could be in your future."

"I'm not looking for fame." Mike smiled. "However a fortune and a good time might be nice."

"Hmm, a good time." Ralphie flipped through the pages with a little too much enthusiasm. The article ripped in half.

Mike watched him piece the halves together. "Anything interesting?"

Ralphie looked up disappointed. "This is a horoscope for the next two months, November and December."

"Exactly," Danny said.

Mike shrugged and walked away to fill his coffee cup. He had finally met a girl he would seriously consider dating, and these two were turning it into some kind of joke. Alex had appealed to him the moment he saw her helping her grandfather unload his van. Her short, quick steps and the sway of her hips had caught his attention. Once she came closer and he saw those big chocolate chip eyes, he knew he was hooked.

Mike had his share of flings. After a dry spell in his social life, it was about time he thought about some kind of lasting relationship. None of his past dates wanted commitment. They were just out for a good time, changing boyfriends as often as they changed the color of their nail polish.

Alex seemed like a down-to-earth kind of girl. He chuckled to himself. As down to earth as she could be with the stars and planets swirling through her head. She seemed to be committed to her grandfather. But the old man could be a problem.

A voice from downstairs broke his train of thought. "Hey, Simone. You up there? There's a pretty little lady with a big box of chocolates asking for you."

Chapter Three

Horoscope: Life can be a production.
Be prepared to deal with it.

For a moment Mike felt as if his thoughts had conjured her arrival. He shook off the silly idea. He glanced at the brass pole. How dramatic would it be if he slid down the pole and presented himself? Too characteristic of a firefighter. What was he thinking? A move like that would most likely turn her right off. He dismissed the notion and took the stairs.

At the bottom of the stairs, Alex waited. He noticed under a navy peacoat she wore hospital scrubs. He smiled at her waif-like appearance in an oversized shirt and baggy pants.

"The ER was busy. They needed an extra pair of hands," she explained. "We had to wait for the plastic surgeon to finish stitching a dog bite." She looked down at the rolled cuffs on her pants. "I started a few IVs and helped discharge some patients while I waited for my grandfather to be treated."

"Your friend the plastic surgeon show up?"

"No, Josh didn't show up. We saw the on-call physician."

Ralphie was right. Josh is a jerk.

Alex seemed uneasy talking about Josh and quickly changed the subject.

"I wanted to apologize for my grandfather's behavior." She thrust a large box, wrapped in pink foil, in his direction. "If you like chocolate, try these."

"I love sweet things." Mike reached for the box. It was heavier than he expected. He locked his fingers around Alex's hand so the box wouldn't slip as she passed it to him. An unexpected spark charged through his arm. His fingers ached to reach over and touch her.

She must have felt the electrifying charge too. Her eyes met his. The look was so galvanizing he felt the muscles in his hands quiver. If this was one of those silly cosmic energies she believed in, he wanted more.

"This is not just any chocolate." She slipped her hands from his grasp and looked at him with wide-open eyes.

Mesmerized by her deep chocolate eyes, he was beginning to believe the power came from the candy. He kept his thought to himself and said, "I can't wait to taste it."

"If you're a true chocolate lover, you'll appreciate Chloe's talent."

"Some kind of secret ingredient?" He looked from the box in his hands to her face.

"Chloe, my grandfather's assistant, perks the chocolate with select spices."

"Spices?" Mike asked.

"Yes." She stared suspiciously at him. "Just spices."

Was she beginning to think like her grandfather. Did she believe that by association, he too was some kind of thief? His interest was purely coincidental. He wondered what this Chloe person and Max did to their chocolates. Pushing his suspicions to the back of his mind, for now, he said, "Sounds different. I'm sure the guys will enjoy them."

"Thank your partner and Ralphie and his team for me."

He sensed her gratitude was genuine. "I'm glad we were so close by." Mike tucked the box of candy under his arm. "If there's anything else I can do, just ask."

"You've already done enough."

"Putting out fires is what I do best," he said in a casual jesting way, then in a more serious tone he asked, "How's your grandfather?"

"He's going to need close follow-up and rest." She released a long exhausted sigh.

"Is he giving you a hard time already?"

"My grandfather is a strong-willed, independent man. He doesn't like being told what he can and cannot do."

Mike kept his thoughts to himself. It appeared Alex inherited more than dark hair and her petite frame from her grandfather. Mike got the impression she too had a

hard time accepting help. He wondered if her horoscope warned her not to accept help from strange men.

"Where is your grandfather now?" Mike asked.

"I took him home."

"He seemed anxious to get back to work. Will you be
able to keep him away from his shop?"

"Nilda offered to stay with him."

"The gypsy?" Mike couldn't imagine an old timer
like Max Martinelli and the Hungarian fortune-teller
had anything in common.

"She's a certified astrologer. She's been my grandfather's friend for many years." Alex had a bemused smile
on her lips. "I know, you're an asparagus. You don't
believe in ascendants or rising stars."

If her dark eyes didn't sparkle with that mischievous
twinkle, Mike might be tempted to reconsider wanting to
ask her out. She seemed deeper than the other girls he
had dated. He had faced bigger challenges in his life than
this petite nurse in baggy scrubs who believed the stars
and planets dictated her life. He was more determined
than before to prove he could change her mind about dating firemen, especially one related to some notorious Simone who had stolen something from her grandfather.

This might be the perfect opportunity to make his
move. "I get off soon. Do you need help bringing the
equipment back to the store?"

"No thanks. Nilda told me the other merchants already packed up Grandpa's van."

Alex was relentless. He wondered if her star sign, or
whatever it was called, made her so stubborn.

One last try and then he'd give up, for now. "Some of that equipment seems pretty heavy. You might need help unloading."

"Well, if you really want to help, I'm too tired to argue," she conceded. "I won't be at the shop until very late. I want to make sure my grandfather is comfortable before I leave again."

"How late?" Mike didn't want to sound like he was backing out but he did have to be on duty at 7 tomorrow morning.

"Is ten too late?"

"Not at all."

Alex rolled her shoulders in what appeared to be to an attempt to relieve today's tension. "The store is on Union Street, between Clinton and Henry," she said.

Mike watched her walk away. Unaware of Mike's scrutiny, she released her hair from the clip that held it in place. Her dark curls fell in graceful waves over the crinkled shoulders of her oversized scrubs. Mike decided what she needed was a strong pair of hands to gently massage away the day's tension. He stood at ease, folded his hands behind his back, and smiled as he watched the gentle sway of her hips that even those baggy scrubs couldn't hide.

Behind him, Mike heard the buzz of the firehouse busybodies. Danny, followed by the paramedics, walked down the stairs. Mike turned and went back into the garage.

"We came up with an idea that might help you win the lady's heart." Danny had a smug look on his face.

"Thanks, guys, but I don't need your help. I'm meeting Alex at the chocolate shop when I'm done here."

"Big deal. You're gonna help her unload the van," Danny said.

"Were you guys listening?"

"We were coming down the stairs. We may have overheard a few words." Ralphie reached for the box of candy. "What'd she bring?"

Mike handed him the box. "Don't spoil your appetite."

Ralphie wasted no time. He ripped the decorative wrapper from the box. "How do you know she'll see you again after tonight?" he asked with his mouth full of chocolate.

"You have a better idea?" Mike hated to admit they were most likely right.

"Read this article. I'm convinced this here is your answer to winning her heart." Danny handed Mike the two halves of the newspaper.

"What am I supposed to do with this?" Mike stared at the words on the page: "While the sun is in the twelfth house . . ."

"This makes no sense." He gave the ripped paper back to Danny.

"Why are you so thick? It's all right there, in front of you." Danny slapped the paper with the back of his hand. "All you have to do is follow her charts, starting the beginning of next month. Read this and you'll know ahead of time when to pull her strings and when not to."

"You guys have lost it. Were you standing too close

to the fire? Did you inhale some toxic fumes and kill some brain cells?" Mike walked around the engine to the other side of the garage.

They went after him.

"Just listen to what Danny has to say." Ralphie blocked Mike's path. He stuffed another truffle in his mouth. "These are very good."

"Alex said they're for everyone." Mike took the box from Ralphie and shoved it into Danny's hand. "Have one."

Danny took two candies and shoved them into his mouth. "Hmm, not bad."

"You guys have no class. These are expensive chocolates, not M&Ms." Mike reached into the box and removed a chocolate. "You've got to savor the flavor." Chewing slowly, he allowed the taste to tease his taste buds while he tried to analyze the ingredients.

The chocolate and its filling melted into an exuberant experience he hadn't expected. He exhaled a long sigh of intense pleasure. If only he could get his frosting to taste like this, none of the other entries at the bake-off would stand a chance.

"Wow. I want one of those." Ralphie took the box away from Danny and began searching for a candy just like Mike had eaten.

With a blend of chili peppers and sweet chocolate lingering on his tongue, Mike leaned against the wall and studied the two halves of the newspaper article. He looked up at the sound of the ladder truck pulling to a screeching halt outside the firehouse.

The driver of the ladder truck left the cab and walked toward them. "What's going on?"

"I'm trying to help Mike out with his love life." Danny waved the top half of the article. "Here. Read this article and tell me what you think."

"Wow. A year of fame, fortune, and a good time," the driver read out loud. "Hey, you got a problem with that, kid."

Still in their smoky bunker gear, the rest of the ladder team gathered around.

In between their whistles and whoops, Danny gave a brief explanation of the events leading up to his plan. "Imagine knowing a woman's fate before she does."

Mike reached for the paper and asked, "How do you expect me to know what will happen to her before she does? It's completely illogical?"

Danny came over and put his arm around Mike. "That's the beauty of this plan. It's the little things. If her horoscope predicts someone will send her flowers, you be the guy who sends them."

"There's one little flaw in this plan," Mike said.

"What flaw?" Danny asked.

"Don't I have to know her birthday before I can read her daily horoscope?"

Danny threw his hands in the air. "Some of this you have to do yourself."

"This is the craziest thing I've heard in a long time." Mike walked away and started up the stairs.

"What's the matter, kid? Afraid you can't do it?" Danny was practically on Mike's heels.

At the top of the stairs, Mike turned and faced the small mob. "Is this a challenge?"

Mike might be considered a senior to some of the new guys, but to most of the old-timers like Danny, he was still a rookie. They no longer sent him off on foolish tasks but liked to bust his chops when it came to the women in his life, which lately had been nonexistent.

Danny stood directly in front of him. "I dare you to follow Alex's horoscope up until the bake-off. It gives you almost four weeks to win her heart." In an exaggerated gesture he placed his open palms over the left side of his chest. "Use your charm and her horoscope to prove she's wasted a lot of time with the wrong men."

Mike considered what Danny had said. It was just a harmless bet with the guys. Alex would never have to know.

"Any conditions or boundaries?" Mike waited while some of the guys, hoping to make the challenge more difficult, tried to think of a few.

"Why, you got any conditions?" Danny asked.

Mike studied the surrounding faces. He had their attention. "Yes, I've got one condition. No one discusses this with any of the merchants in the neighborhood." He envisioned the wildfire of gossip that could spread if this challenge jumped from the lips of one shopkeeper to the next. "I mean no one."

"Our lips are sealed. We won't tell the butcher, the baker, or even the chocolate-maker." Danny threw back his head and laughed. "We wouldn't want to embarrass you if you fail."

Mike was beyond intimidation. He looked Danny straight in his eyes and said, "Don't worry about me. By the end of the month, Miss Martinelli will realize she's been dating all the wrong men." He took charge. "She'll realize she should have hooked a Simone a long time ago."

"Oh, to be young and confident." Danny chuckled. "Want the terms in writing?"

"I don't want you to have to strain yourself. Our verbal agreement is just as binding." Mike extended his hand.

"I knew you couldn't resist the challenge." Danny clasped Mike's hand in a firm handshake. He leaned closer and added quietly, "I can tell you really like this girl. Good luck."

Mike hated to admit he would need more than luck. Though he felt an equal attraction on her part, he knew he had to act soon. By accepting the challenge, the guys were forcing him to follow through.

Alex did not seem like the type to fall head over heels, and flowers and candy would definitely not impress her. First, though, he needed a surefire way to get close enough to find out her birthday or the bet was off.

He glanced at the date on his watch, October 29. He had less than three days to find out Alex's sign.

Chapter Four

Horoscope: Take advantage of the little things in life.

Alex drove the van slowly down Union Street. With the kind of day she had, she doubted she would be lucky enough to find a parking spot close to the store. As she cruised past the shop, a man waved at her.

Dressed in jeans and a bomber jacket, Mike Simone looked out of place under the pink CHOCOLATE BOUTIQUE sign. Seeing him there promptly at ten minutes before ten had caught her a little off guard. Maybe she was just too used to Josh. Josh and his million-and-one excuses why he had never been on time for anything.

Her life was beginning to sound like a horoscope reading. *Everything hits at once but take advantage of the little things.* She supposed most people would consider the

sudden appearance of a good-looking fireman something to be grateful for.

Occupied with her thoughts, she almost missed a great
parking spot. She smiled. A parking spot on a busy
Brooklyn Street was definitely one of the little rewards
in life. As she prepared to parallel park, she realized it
would be a tight squeeze for the big van.

She checked the sideview mirror. Mike had come
alongside. Was that a cake box in his hand? He motioned with his free hand in a counter-clockwise direction. She followed his signal and turned the steering
wheel away from the curb.

The back tires hit the curb. "Oh, chocolate stars."
Alex smacked the steering wheel with her open palms.
She'd never get this monster into that little spot.

"You've got it. Just turn in the opposite direction."
Mike stood outside the window. He gave her a smile
that sent her heart racing.

She took a deep breath and adjusted her hands. With
relative ease the van slipped into the vacant spot with
only inches to spare.

She turned off the engine and stepped out of the van.
"Thanks. You seem to be showing up at all the right
times today."

"I usually try to limit my rescues to one per lady in
distress for the day."

"Then I'll consider myself special." She nodded at
the box in his hand. "What's in the box?"

"Your cake. You did pay for it. I'd really like you to
taste a slice."

"Why me?"

"There's something missing in my chocolate frosting. I thought since you grew up surrounded by chocolate, you might have some suggestions."

"I'm flattered but you've got the wrong Martinelli." She walked around to the back of the van. She didn't have the heart to tell him that his lopsided creation didn't look all that appealing.

"That's too bad. I don't think your grandfather likes me enough to offer any suggestions." Mike followed her. With the box still in his hand he leaned casually against the door.

"You're right. He doesn't like you." The minute the words passed her lips she realized he hadn't done anything to deserve such a blatant response.

"Can't you put in a good word?"

Alex could talk herself blue but her grandfather would never agreed to help anyone named Simone. "It'll never happen." She turned away before his appealing smile melted her defenses. She opened the door of the van. The minty smell of peppermint diluted the acrid smell of Grandpa's charred cauldron.

Alex rested her hand on the discolored rim. "What a shame, the pot is ruined." It hurt her to see the pot in such a sorry state. There wasn't much they could do to salvage it.

Mike leaned into the van for a better look. "Let me carry it inside." He shook his head regretfully.

She appreciated his offer. She would never be able to move it on her own. She balanced the cake box on her arm and unlocked the door to the store. Mike carried the cumbersome kettle as if it were weightless and followed her inside.

"Where do you want this?" He searched for a place to rest the stinky pot.

"Follow me." Alex headed toward the back of the store.

Mike stopped to look at the chocolate display. The shelves were filled with an assortment of candies, as well as nuts, dried fruit, and pretzels, all covered in chocolate. Resisting the twirling aroma from the display case was a challenge few people could handle.

"Go ahead, try a chocolate," she suggested.

"I wouldn't know which one to take. They all look so tempting."

"What's your preference? Do you like your chocolate sweet or bittersweet?"

"I'm usually a Milky Way, Snickers kind of guy, but those truffles you brought to the firehouse were something else." He looked up from the chocolate selection and studied her. "What do you like?"

Oh, she thought and made a quick appraisal of his features. Dark hair, eyes the color of blue jeans, and tanned chiseled features. Yes, that was exactly what she liked.

"You'll like the dark chocolate. She reached into the case and picked up one of Chloe's artistic chocolates. "Try this."

"Smells delicious. It's too pretty to eat." Mike dipped his chin in the direction of the cauldron he held in his hands. His muscles tensed from the weight of the pot but there was no place to rest it.

"Chloe, Max's chocolate chef likes her creations to appeal to all the senses. You might want to consider that with your cake."

"It is a little lopsided. Isn't it?"

Alex had insulted him once and she didn't want to do it again. She shrugged and placed the chocolate in Mike's mouth. The brief touch of his lips on her fingertips created an unexpected ripple of heat. She saw something intense ignite in his eyes. It was obvious there was a physical pull between them. If her fingers lingered a moment longer a simple spark might kindle an error in her judgment that could prove to be dangerous. She pulled away.

"You'll get a better taste of the chocolate if you don't squish the center with your first bite," she said.

"Hmm." His expression stilled and grew serious as he concentrated on chewing.

She watched him savor the blend of flavors. His sensuous expression told her that she had chosen the right combination. She imagined the chocolate melting lusciously in his mouth. A small smudge of chocolate had stained her finger. She couldn't resist putting it to her lips. An unexpected jolt cascaded through her body. Shocked by her response, she turned her attention back to the display case. Her shaking hands would not allow her to rearrange the remaining candies.

Not a moment too soon the bell rang. The spell was

broken. Someone had entered the store. Alex glanced over the counter to see who it was.

It was Chloe. "What's with this weather?" She pulled off her mittens and rubbed her hands together.

"Chloe, what are you doing here?" Alex left Mike holding the pot and walked over to greet the young woman with spiked hair the color of a cherry lollipop.

Chloe unwrapped the scarf from her neck and removed her cotton candy-colored fake fur bomber jacket.

Alex smiled at her mix-matched friend. She noticed Mike's curious glance. He looked Chloe over with an amused smile on his face. People who knew Chloe associated the unconventional twenty-five-year-old's style and sensitivity with her artistic ability. Alex didn't want to imagine what Mike was thinking of their unexpected visitor.

Unlike most people, Alex didn't find anything odd about Chloe. She had a heart as soft as a mushy chocolate center. Her quirky fashion sense and her ability to read people and situations was not a trait often seen in girls her age. Alex attributed Chloe's style and emotional intelligence not only to the time she spent with her elderly Aunt Bessie, but her parents as well. Her parents were archaeologists who sent Chloe packages from strange and exotic locations.

Max allowed Chloe to display only the artifacts used for chocolate making on a wall above the counter. Chloe had convinced Max that some of these objects held ancient chocolate-making secrets.

When Max had hired Chloe three years ago, fresh out

of culinary school, he had his doubts about her experience in the business. It was just around the time Alex's grandmother, Gladys, had become too ill to work. Quirky but talented, Chloe quickly learned every nook and cranny of the shop and displayed a remarkable skill with chocolate blends, becoming a vital part of the business and the family.

"Shouldn't you be home in bed, nursing that cold?" Alex took Chloe by the elbow and ushered her away from the door.

"Don't worry about me." With her soft, artistic hands, she held the side of Alex's face and kissed her on the forehead. "You look like you had a rough day, girlfriend." She glanced past her and asked, "Who's this?"

"Chloe, this is Mike."

Chloe extended an arm full of jingling bangles, then snapped it away. "What happened to Max's pot?"

"You haven't heard?" Alex was sure the news about the incident at the candy booth had already spread through the neighborhood's gossip network.

It was obvious by the shocked expression on Chloe's face that she had no idea that Max had burned his hand.

Alex explained in short, fragmented sentences. "There was a fire. The cauldron was destroyed. Mike's a firefighter. He helped contain the fire and offered to help unload the van."

Tired and anxious to get home, Alex didn't want to relive all the events of the morning. Chloe would just have to wait until later. When they were alone she would fill her in on all the events of the day. Alex glanced at Mike, his muscles straining against the weight of the pot. There were some things Chloe would not need to know.

"Well, don't leave this poor man standing here." Chloe motioned toward the back of the store. "Take that horrid thing out of my sight."

She gave Alex a sideways glance as they followed Mike. She knew Chloe's curious look required some kind of explanation. "I told you he's a firefighter, who luckily for us, happened to be at the fair," Alex said.

"Yeah, and?" Chloe waited for her to continue.

"And nothing." Alex replied and opened the door to the back of the store. A magical feeling always filled the place where her grandfather's delicate candy took shape.

Chloe followed on Alex's heels and hit the light switch. As she walked by, she mumbled loud enough for only Alex to hear. "He just happened to show up here tonight?"

"Chloe, I know what you're thinking. He's a nice guy who was just being kind to an old man."

"And his single, unattached granddaughter."

"He doesn't know that." Alex shrugged. "If that's his intention, I haven't noticed."

"Okay, you're not talking. I'll go see what else I can salvage from the van." She buttoned her jacket and walked away, leaving Alex alone with Mike.

Alex watched Chloe walk away. She turned her attention back to Mike, who seemed at a loss as to where to place the burnt pot. All the work counters were scrubbed clean and shiny. For a moment she wasn't sure the damaged cauldron belonged in the store. On the far wall she noticed an empty shelf and guided Mike toward it. He squatted with the cumbersome pot in his arms while she stood behind him.

When he stood, he turned and faced her. Alex found herself wedged on each side by a counter and the shelves. Mike was directly in front of her, so close she could still smell the creamy chocolate on his breath. The muscles in his arms had relaxed when he placed the pot securely on the shelf. She resisted the urge to reach up and rest her hand on his strong arm.

He inhaled a deep breath and said, "I didn't realize how heavy that thing was." He made no effort to move away so she could pass.

She tried to relax and think of something witty to say. Nothing came to mind. Instead she found herself studying his face with his compelling eyes and the touch of humor around his lips. Out of his uniform, it was easy to forget he was a firefighter. Something inside her started to melt like chocolate exposed to heat.

Needing to create a little space between them, she placed her open palms on his chest. She felt his muscles quiver beneath her fingers. She pulled away at the same moment he stepped back, almost toppling the shelves behind him.

As if on cue, Chloe returned. "Oh no!" Her arms flailed in the air as they often did when she was excited. "The doctor is coming."

"Doctor? What doctor?" Alex turned. She could still sense Mike directly behind her.

"Your ex-doctor. I mean your ex-husband, Josh."

"Josh? He's here now. What for?"

"Did I hear my name?" Josh stepped into the already overcrowded work area. He looked from Mike to Alex and glared at Chloe, who was slipping out the door.

"It just got very cold in here." Chloe peeked in from around the doorframe, only her eyes and the spikes of her hair were visible. "Anyone want some hot cocoa?"

"Sounds great," Mike said. "Let me help you. He maneuvered between Alex and the counter. In a gesture that was both deliberate and reassuring, he placed his hands on her shoulders.

Through the fabric of her sweater, she felt the strong comforting grasp of his fingers. With a slight tilt of her head, she looked up. "We'll join you in a minute."

Josh paced back and forth in the small room while he waited for everyone extraneous to leave.

Alex was not in the mood to hear any of his elaborate apologies for not treating her grandfather. However, she was curious as to why he was here, now.

"What are you doing here?" she asked.

"I might ask you the same question. I walk in and find you in a compromising position with some strange man."

"Compromising position? He's not a strange man. He's a firefighter. He helped my grandfather today." Alex could hear her voice rising with each short sentence. "Did you forget we're not married anymore? What gives you the right to tell me who I should or should not be with?"

"Listen, Alex," Josh reached for her hands, "You have to know I still care about you."

Alex fidgeted with some lollipop sticks. She usually performed best under pressure, but seeing Josh always made her think of her biological clock and how much she had wanted to be a parent and how adamant Josh had been about the time never being right. At first he wanted to focus on his career. Once he became successful he hardly had time for Chloe, nevermind a family.

"Let's go have our chocolate before it gets cold." She turned on her heels. The clock on the wall read 11:00. The day was almost over. She'd already dealt with her share of crises for one day. Alex headed for the front of the store, not caring if Josh followed her or not.

The group seated around the bistro-style table was an odd mix. Mike, with his neat military-style haircut, had straddled the little chair. The soft, peppermint-striped cushion yielded to his weight. Josh, with his perfectly placed hair, leaned back in his seat with his arms crossed over his chest. Chloe, with her red spikes, poured her steamy chocolate blend into oversized white mugs and waited for everyone to take a sip.

A taste of the soothing blend was just what they needed to soften everyone's mood. Alex decided this might also be the perfect time to sample Mike's cake. She cut small slices and explained, "Mike made this cake. He'd like our opinion." She passed the first slice to Josh, hoping to soften his sour expression.

"None for me." Josh stopped her with an open palm.

"You made this cake?" Chloe tilted her head to adjust to the angle of the cake. "I hope it tastes better than it looks."

"Yes. I'd like to enter it in the firefighters bake-off but something is missing. The guys at the house think it's good but I can't trust their judgment."

"Not very nice to look at, but that's easy to change. Lets see how it tastes." Chloe dug her fork into the piece in front of her. She was silent while she analyzed the taste.

Alex copied her move, gathering the frosting and cake on her fork. The cake was perfect. So good she almost forgot the appearance. The frosting was creamy but didn't complement the cake. She was about to tell Mike her thoughts when Josh broke the silence.

"So, you're a firefighter." Josh's mouth spread into a thin-lipped smile. "Do you live in the neighborhood?"

"Not far. I live in Park Slope." Mike took a sip of his cocoa, then cradled the mug in his hands.

"I didn't think you guys made the kind of money to afford those rents." Josh stirred his hot cocoa a little too vigorously.

"My parents own a brownstone on Pineapple Street. Moving back in with them was a matter of economics when I got accepted to the fire academy." Mike took another sip of his chocolate. "They travel a lot now. I keep an eye on the place and get a great place to live."

Alex stood up and walked over to Josh. With a clean towel she wiped up the mess around his cup.

"Just like Alex." Josh hooked his hand around her waist. "Do you know she still lives in the same house she grew up in? It's prime real estate now." He tightened his fingers possessively. "She lives there with her grandfather, Max." He looked up at Alex with the confidence that he knew more about her than the stranger across the table.

Alex wiggled free from Josh's tense grasp. Josh had chosen to leave out an important detail regarding her current living situation. Josh had gotten their condo as part of the divorce agreement. On a nurse's salary she couldn't afford the expensive maintenance fees she and Josh had paid together.

"My parents are snowbirds. They go to Florida for the winter. Grandpa Max refuses to leave the store and go with them." She glared at Josh, then looked at Mike and smiled. "Like you, I found myself in an economic crunch and moved in with my grandfather."

"My parents usually trek down to Boca Raton for the winters, but this year they're sticking around for the holidays," Mike said.

"You two seem to have a lot in common," Josh mumbled.

Gracefully sinking into the soft cushion on the chair between Mike and Josh, Alex reached for her cup. She took a long slow sip of her hot cocoa. Over the rim of her cup, she watched Josh. He hadn't touched his beverage or his cake. Maybe a sip of Chloe's comforting brew would release the tense look on his face.

Behind the mound of whipped cream, Alex couldn't

help smiling. She could almost smell the testosterone in the air. Only Chloe had nothing to say. She was still trying to determine what was wrong with the frosting on Mike's cake.

Josh continued to pry into Mike's life. "So, do you have generations of firemen in your family or were they cake bakers?"

Alex took a sip of her hot cocoa and listened. She hoped Mike would shed some light on her grandfather's hostility toward the Simones.

"Actually my family is in construction. My grandfather started a small company out of Red Hook." There was pride in Mike's tone as he spoke about his family's struggle to build the business into the successful firm it was today.

Alex noticed the confidence in Mike's voice. Josh was confident too, but in a cocky, self-indulgent way. There was definitely something attractive in Mike's self-assurance. He knew how to take charge while maintaining his proper place.

"Is your father retired?" Josh asked.

"He likes to think he is," Mike laughed.

"Who runs the business while you're busy putting out fires?" Josh seemed annoyed by Mike's cool, joking manner.

"My sisters." Mike's tone changed, indicating this time he wasn't amused.

Alex noticed the lines around his blue eyes deepened. She wondered if Josh had touched on a sensitive subject.

"Big, healthy girls I assume." Josh snickered.

"Actually my sister Kate is petite like Alex. She's got an MBA from Wharton, but when she shows up on a job site no one would dare cross her or she'd fire them on the spot." Mike looked Josh straight in the eye.

Josh stared back. Alex played with her empty cup unsure how to break the silence.

Chloe came to the rescue. She jumped up from her seat saving the moment with her shouts. "I've got it! The cake is wonderful, sweet and moist, in spite of its somewhat uneven appearance." She waved her fork at Mike. "But the frosting, something is missing. It does nothing to enhance the flavors or appearance of the wonderful cake underneath."

Mike leaned forward. "What do you think it needs?"

"Of course a more pleasant presentation would help, but not as much as my special chocolate blend," Chloe said.

"Sounds simple. I'm sure I can fix it if you'd share the recipe with me."

"Oh no. I can't do that." Chloe shook his head. "It's not mine to give."

"You just told the guy you have some kind of chocolate blend." Josh seemed anxious for this conversation to end. "Just give it to him," he demanded.

Chloe glared at Josh, her face as bright as the frosted tips of her hair. "It's my creation but it belongs to Max too. He's been burnt before," Chloe raised a brow and smiled at Mike. "Excuse the pun, but Max is very secretive about our recipes."

"Oh, that whole Simone chocolate thing," Mike said.

"How do you know about those thieves?" Chloe stiffened.

"Your boss seemed to think I might be a descendent of this Simone guy he had a run-in with."

"Why would he think such a horrid thought?" Chloe asked.

Alex realized she had only used Mike's first name in her introduction earlier. "Because his name is Mike Simone." The words were no more than a whisper.

"You're a Simone?" Chloe inhaled and grabbed her chest. "Is he?" She looked at Alex.

"That's his last name." Alex couldn't believe a lopsided chocolate cake with bad frosting had started such a commotion. "I never understood that whole Simone thing until this morning when my grandfather told us how Mike's uncle stole his secret recipe."

"Max told you?" Chloe seemed surprised.

"He was very upset when he found out that Mike was related to Sal Simone." Remembering how her grandfather spoke to Mike, Alex gave him an apologetic glance.

"He seems like a nice guy but . . ." Chloe looked at Alex and sighed. "I wish I could help him." She started to place the mugs on a tray. When she reached for Mike's, she hesitated. "Maybe Max will come to his senses and forget this ridiculous feud."

Mike stood, a handsome, self-confident presence. He seemed untouched by Chloe's refusal to help him. "I guess I better be going. Thanks for the hot chocolate. It was really extraordinary." He acknowledged Chloe with a nod. "I'll work on my chocolate."

"Too bad you can't get the frosting to work." The sarcasm in Josh's voice was as thick as fudge.

Mike ignored Josh and turned to Alex. "Is there anything else I can do before I leave?"

"I'm sure Alex has everything under control," Josh answered, then looked over at Alex. "Don't you?"

"Mike's been more than kind. Now that you're here to help I don't think we need to bother him anymore." She gave Josh a coy smile.

"Absolutely." Josh rolled his napkin. "What else needs to be done?"

"The dishes need to be cleaned." She helped Chloe stack the dirty cups.

Josh looked at his hands. "I've got surgery tomorrow."

"I'm sure I can find you a pair of gloves," Alex said.

"They'll have to be Latex-free."

"It figures," Chloe mumbled under her breath as Josh walked away.

Alex had no energy left for this petty situation. "Just forget it," she said and turned her attention to Mike. "Thanks for all your help."

"I'm glad I was there." His tone was sincere, filled with warmth and concern. "You're going to need some rest. Don't hang out here and aggravate yourself." He looked over her shoulder at Josh.

"I'll lock the door behind you." She left Josh sitting at the table and followed Mike to the front of the shop. "Don't pay attention to Josh."

"I didn't pay him any mind and I think you shouldn't either." He brushed a loose strand of hair from her cheek. "By the way, what's your sign?"

She hadn't expected his fingers to be so smooth. "My sign?" It took several seconds for his words to register.

"Yes, you know, asparagus, radish, radicchio." Her surprise seemed to amuse him.

"I'm a Scorpio," she laughed in answer.

"Ouch, sounds dangerous."

"Not really. Scorpions just have an image problem. We have a lot to live up to."

"What's it take to avoid the sting?" he asked.

There it was again, that playful curve at the corner of his lips.

"Patience and a good heart."

"I've got both."

"Really. I didn't know those were the traits of an asparagus," she laughed.

"They are. You should check your charts or books or wherever it is you find that kind of information." The sexy tilt at the corner of his lips turned into a big smile. Then he turned and walked out the door.

Alex stood by the window and watched Mike walk away. What was his sudden interest in her star sign? Lost in her thoughts, she didn't realize Josh had come up behind her until she felt his fingers kneading her shoulders. With an unexpected startle she pulled away. She felt no comfort in his touch.

Josh asked, "Why was Simone here tonight? I don't

believe that nonsense about wanting to improve his frosting."

"He helped my grandfather after the fire at the fair."

"A friend of Max's? It sounds like Max would never have a friend with the last name Simone." He gave her a puzzled look. "Anyway, I thought most of Max's friends were octogenarians." A muscle tensed at his jaw.

She turned away so Josh couldn't see the expression on her face. She remembered the sizzling sensation she felt when her fingers touched Mike's lips and the way his eyes had her riveted in place at the candy counter. She didn't want to talk about the way Mike looked at her with anyone, especially Josh.

"You never did tell me why you stopped by tonight," Alex said.

"I called your house and your grandfather told me you were at the chocolate shop. I was on my way home when I got a call from one of the nurses at my surgical center. She has a family emergency. She won't be in all of next week."

Alex looked up at him in disbelief. "You stopped by to ask me if I'm available to work at your surgical center?"

"I thought it was a better idea than asking over the phone."

"Do you have any idea what today has been like? What the rest of my week will be like?" She threw her hands in the air.

"Just say you'll do it." A corner of his thin lips turned up into a pleading smile.

Alex stood there speechless. The nerve of him. Their divorce had been final for over a year now. She owed him nothing. He couldn't find the time to treat her grandfather in the ER. And yet he expected her to juggle her schedule as well as her grandfather's physical therapy and whirlpool appointments just to help him out. How dare he be so presumptuous!

Josh had his back to her and appeared to be studying the candy display. "I should probably place an order for the office for Thanksgiving. Those truffles look unbelievable."

She allowed her temper to cool before answering him. Josh's surgical practice included outpatient centers in all five boroughs of New York City. If the office staff liked these truffles, they would buy more. It could make up for the business lost from the fair.

"Call Chloe during the week. It's been a long day and everyone needs to get home." She grabbed Josh's coat, tossed it at him, and nudged him out the door.

"Just tell me you'll think about picking up some shifts." The door slammed behind him.

"No way," she said out loud even though Josh was already halfway down the street.

She walked back to the table. Chloe had settled things in the back of the store and was preparing to leave.

"Do you want me to wait while you lock up?" she asked.

"No thanks. I'll be fine. You go home and get some rest." She reached up and adjusted the collar of Chloe's fake fur jacket.

"I like your firefighter," Chloe said. "I wish I could help him, but you know how your grandfather is."

"Is there more to the story than what my grandfather told me?"

"All I know is some guy named Simone stole a chocolate recipe and Max hates all Simones, even your firefighter."

"He's not my firefighter." Confused by her torn alliances, Alex felt a bit of regret.

"Whatever." Chloe gave her an evasive shrug and changed the subject. "What's with Josh?" she asked.

"You mean why is he still a part of my life? I keep asking myself the same question."

Chloe nodded. There was no need for words. Alex knew exactly what her friend was asking.

She struggled for a moment with the uncertainty of how her feeble excuse would sound when she actually told someone. "It's me. Sometimes I think I'm not emotionally ready to give up Josh completely. I guess it's because we go back a long time. We knew each other in high school." She sighed and sank into the chair. "How pathetic does that sound?"

"Pretty bad," Chloe said. "I think he's hoping you'll get back together."

"Don't worry. It won't happen in this lifetime."

After Chloe left, Alex stared out the window. The street was quiet except for a few stragglers going home after a late dinner. She remembered when walking down Smith Street at night wasn't safe. *Things do change,* she thought. Now the street was lined with sidewalk cafes and funky boutiques. It had been awhile since she had a normal date and walked down any street late at night.

Stop feeling sorry for yourself, she thought as she gathered her coat and pocketbook. Inhaling deeply she hoped to clear her mind of everything Josh had said. Surprisingly, her senses filled not with the lingering scent of Josh's expensive cologne but with a familiar smell. The smell her father and brothers had brought home from the firehouse.

She found comfort in the smoky scent that lingered after Mike Simone, the asparagus.

Chapter Five

Horoscope: Open your mind to amorous adventure.

Alex sat in the staff lounge and stared at the nurse's schedule for the next month. The upcoming schedule included Christmas and New Years. She couldn't believe the holidays were just around the corner.

Even before her grandfather's accident, she had planned to take time off around the holidays. He always needed extra help for the season, but recent circumstances made it important that she get the time off. She'd ask for family leave time if she needed to. They'd know soon if Grandpa Max would be able to return to work.

She walked over to the microwave and heated up water for tea. The bell no longer worked on the overused machine, so she watched the cup until the water cascaded over the rim. She removed the mug and placed a tea bag into the steamy bubbles.

When the water turned to dark amber, she removed the bag and let it hang over the cup for a few seconds. As she watched the drips hit the surface and vanish, her thoughts drifted. Who would have ever thought her day off would have ended the way it did.

After the hectic weekend, she was glad to be back at work. The ER was short-staffed and patients were being held because the floors had no beds open for new admissions. In spite of the craziness, Alex preferred the hectic ER to the events of the past weekend. Luckily, her brothers had offered to share the responsibility of getting their grandfather back and forth to his many appointments. Even Chloe offered to chauffeur Max around, but it was more important for her to have everything under control at the shop.

With everything under control, why did Alex feel so off balance? Did her unharmonious feelings have anything to do with that handsome Mike Simone? Chances were slim she'd run into him again anytime soon. Chloe had been firm that she would not divulge her chocolate recipe, and it was obvious that Grandpa couldn't stand the sight of anyone named Simone. Mike seemed like the kind of guy who didn't need to be told twice.

Breaktime was over. Recollections of the weekend were pushed to the back of her mind. Out of habit, she walked by the bulletin board and removed the OR schedule. Josh had an early morning case. A scar revision, something he preferred not to perform at the surgery center. As far as she was concerned, the Josh issue was resolved. She had no intention of working in his outpatient center. She pressed the schedule back on the board. The tack left an imprint on her thumb.

Alex was about to reach for the newspaper and quickly read her horoscope when the unit secretary's voice echoed over the intercom. "Alex, please locate. The patient in room four needs her nurse."

Alex smiled. The patient in room four, Sadie Bell was a Monday-morning frequent flyer. The staff suspected she spent the weekend with her children and the Monday-morning loneliness was more than the elderly lady could bear. She'd show up in the ER with an assortment of complaints. Alex folded the newspaper and placed it on the table. Her horoscope would have to wait.

Behind the curtain to bed four, Alex found Mrs. Bell propped up with pillows. Alex had never seen so many pillows in the ER. Leave it to Sadie to get someone to position her like a queen. Her breakfast tray sat untouched by the bedside. Serving meals to ER patients was a recent addition to the staffs' already-heavy duties. It had come about as a result of patient satisfaction surveys.

"Are you the person I complain to?" The older woman waved a piece of burnt toast in the air.

"Sure. What's the problem?" Alex smiled.

"This toast. How can you expect a sick person to eat something like this?" She scraped the knife across the top of the bread, sending a flurry of charcoal all over her eggs.

"How about I get you a whole new breakfast?" Alex

fluffed the pillows. "When you're done, I'll bring you your blood pressure medicine."

"Good, that's I why come to this hospital. You know how to treat your patients." With her palms Mrs. Bell smoothed the wrinkles from her sheets. "But your linen is still a little too rough."

Alex picked up the tray and left the room. At the nurses station she stopped and said, "You gotta love this job."

"Was it Mrs. Bell in room four?" Lise, the unit secretary asked. "What was it now? The eggs, the coffee, the sheets?"

"Her toast." Alex handed Lise the tray. "Can you run over to the kitchen and get her a new breakfast? I'll call and tell them you're on your way."

County was a big municipal hospital. The ER was in the *A* building and the kitchen was over in the *B* building. By the time Lise went there and back, there was a good chance Mrs. Bell would be discharged. Alex walked to the medication room to get Sadie's blood pressure pills.

Alex was in charge today, and she knew what was happening with every patient in the emergency room. Because of the sick calls, she had to take a light assignment. She could only hope the day didn't progress in the wrong direction. She knew better than to even think the word *quiet*. It was always a bad omen if someone, even accidentally, said the word out loud. Maybe she should have taken a few seconds to check her horoscope. Mrs. Bell's toast could have waited.

With the pills in her hand, Alex stepped behind the curtain to room four. Sadie didn't look happy. Her nose was turned up and she sniffed the air.

"Everything okay?" The minute the words were out of her mouth Alex was sorry she had asked.

"I don't think so," Mrs. Bell said.

"Are you not feeling well?" Alex asked.

"I'm much better, dear." The older woman inhaled deeply. "Something's wrong. Don't you smell the smoke?"

"Smoke?" Alex stepped outside the cubicle and sniffed. Mrs. Bell was right. Something was burning. She peaked back around the curtain and reassured the old lady. "I'm sure it's nothing. I'll go check."

Alex increased her pace as she hurried toward the nurses station. Overhead the operator announced, "Code red. Basement laundry."

Even during routine drills, hallways were cleared and fire doors closed. Maybe it was the faint smell of smoke that had the staff reacting with a little more urgency. By the time Alex reached the desk, she was sure this wasn't a drill. The assortment of people in suits that had congregated in the small space confirmed her belief.

Dr. Frank, the medical director, approached. "Smoke is starting to come up through the back vents in the supply room. We have to prepare to move patients," he said.

"Move patients?" Alex looked at him as if he was crazy. "Where are we going to move them?"

"A horizontal evacuation."

Alex understood what a horizontal evacuation was. The patients closest to the smoke, like Sadie, would move one compartment away. The only problem was, the ER was a big open corridor. That meant the patients would have to move out of the building. Her stomach did a flip.

Dr. Frank placed a reassuring hand on her shoulder. "I'll call dispatch and tell them we're on diversion." His voice held an edge of urgency. "They'll send us any available paramedic units to help with the move." He gave her an understanding look before he stepped away to call 911.

"Let's see who we can discharge." Alex gathered up the charts. She had already compiled a mental list of the patients and their conditions. "The patients waiting for beds will have to go to area hospitals."

"EMS is aware of the situation." Dr. Frank was back by her side. "Give me a quick assessment of the patients, and we'll start moving."

On her other side, the nurse manager took her by the arm. "We have to move everyone outside to the ambulance area."

Alex nodded in agreement. There was no visible sign of smoke or fire but the smell was getting stronger. She and the staff knew what had to be done. Fortunately, they had participated in numerous disaster drills. What appeared uncontrolled to outsiders was really organized chaos. Everyone had a job to do.

"Anything I can do to help?" A familiar male voice asked from behind.

Alex turned, surprised to find Josh in his surgical scrubs leaning casually against the desk. She didn't answer right away. Regaining her composure she asked, "What are you doing here?"

"My nine o'clock surgery was canceled because of this commotion." He leaned close and asked in a whisper, "Is there really a fire?"

"In the basement."

"Well, I'm here to help." There was an edge of reluctance in his voice.

Alex knew Josh would not feel bad if she dismissed his generous offer. She didn't. They would need all available hands.

"Don't go far." She turned her attention back to the patients being moved into wheelchairs.

An aide wheeled Mrs. Bell by the desk. "Hurry, dear. There's a fire," the old woman said.

Alex recognized the aide, Ralphie, one of the fire rescue people who picked up extra time in the ER.

She grabbed him by the arm. "I'm glad you're working today. Let Josh, Dr. Pratt, take this patient outside. I need you to help move equipment and supplies." She took the handles of the wheelchair and turned them in Josh's direction. "This is Sadie Bell. Can you escort her outside, please?"

Josh obediently followed her command. As they started to move away she added, "And check her blood pressure when you get a chance."

Over his shoulder Josh looked at Alex. He had a skeptical tilt to his lips.

"You do know how to inflate a blood pressure cuff, don't you?" Alex was amused by the unsure look on his face.

Josh was about to answer when Mrs. Bell reached up and patted his hand. "Don't worry, Doc. I'll show you how it's done." The older woman looked Josh over from head to toe. "What kind of doctor are you? A surgeon?"

"I'm a plastic surgeon." He rolled his eyes at Alex.

"I'm sure you're very good at what you do or you wouldn't be on staff here." Mrs. Bell gave Josh her vote of confidence.

Alex knew Sadie was right. Josh was an excellent surgeon. There was a time when he had had a smooth bedside manner too. He would need a lot of that charm now. Mrs. Bell was about to give him an earful concerning her surgical history.

"Hurry up and get outside," he said to Alex as he rounded the corner of the desk.

"As soon as I can," Alex shouted after him. She watched the back of Josh's head bobbing up and down in response to Mrs. Bell's continuous chatter.

"What equipment do you want outside?" Ralphie asked.

Alex realized he was talking to her and turned her attention back to her task. "Let's take our crash cart and some IV supplies. The paramedic teams should have what we need in their ambulances. Do you think your firehouse will respond?"

"The hospital's not in their area but they could be special called. It's a pretty big complex. If the fire is hard to contain we could have a dangerous situation on our hands."

"Let's hope that doesn't happen." Alex prepared the crash cart to be moved. She handed Ralphie the supplies that had accumulated on top. "Is Simone on today?" She tried to sound nonchalant.

"I'm pretty sure I saw his name on the board when I signed out this morning."

Something about Ralphie's smile made her sorry she asked the question. The last thing she wanted was for anyone to think she was remotely interested in the handsome firefighter. She turned toward the blanket warmer and removed some heated blankets to take with her.

Outside, Alex was surprised by the unseasonably warm autumn day. A gentle breeze blew from the south. Police cars and fire trucks had blocked off the access to incoming vehicles. Around the corner of the building the firefighters pulled on their boots and rubber coats as they prepared to enter through the side door. Dressed in full bunker gear, with air packs on their backs and their face masks ready, they disappeared into the smoky corridors while everyone else was clearing the lower floors of the building.

She spotted Mrs. Bell and Josh off to the side of the crowded ambulance ramp. She hurried over to see if Josh had survived his ordeal.

"Well, dear, your ex-husband did a fine job." Mrs. Bell removed the blood pressure cuff. The flesh on her upper arm jiggled as the cuff unfolded. "My pressure is fine."

Alex glared at Josh and wondered what he had told the old lady. Behind her she heard the pumper being hooked up to the fire hydrant. She turned and watched a firefighter take the nozzle. She could see the strain on his face as he pulled a length of hose over his shoulder. This was not the time to worry about what Josh had said about their relationship.

She turned her attention back to Sadie. The numbers on the electronic blood pressure machine were within an acceptable range for a woman Sadie's age. Alex turned to the old lady and smiled. "I'm glad to see you responded to the medication. You're stable enough to go home. I'll send someone over to help discharge you." She took Sadie's wrinkled hand and offered to help her up from the wheelchair.

"No, dear, no. I can't go."

"Of course, you can. Everything is fine." Alex looked at Josh for confirmation. "Isn't she fine, Dr. Pratt?"

"She's in better shape than some of my patients half her age."

"It's not my condition." There was an edge of panic in Sadie's voice. "It's my pocketbook. I left it inside. I can't go any place without it."

"Your pocketbook?" Alex wanted to laugh. "Don't worry. I'll find someone to get it for you." She looked around. There was no one to ask. "I'll be right back." She started to walk back toward the ER.

"Where do you think you're going?" Josh reached out and grabbed her shoulder.

"You know how old ladies are about their pocket-books. They carry their lives in them."

"I don't think it's a good idea to be running into a burning building for some old lady's purse."

"The building is not burning. I just came from inside and there's only a faint smell of smoke in the hall. The fire is in the basement." She looked at Josh and smiled. She realized this was his strange way of saying he cared. "Wait here. I'll be right back."

Mike had been sitting around the table having break-fast with the guys from his team and the ladder company when the call came in on the telephone. The hospital operator had called in the fire. After calling to verify the address and location, the house officer wrote the in-formation on the board. "County Hospital!" he shouted above the chatter.

Everyone scrambled for their gear. The engine was on the street in less than forty-five seconds.

Mike stuck his head out the window of the cab when the tall tower of County came into view. He tightened his grip on the door as the driver took a sharp turn into the hospital parking lot. He remembered that Alex had said she was working today. They waited for the police to clear a path for the engine before they were able to pull up close to the building.

The scene looked like mass chaos. Medical equip-ment, ambulances, patients on stretchers and seated in wheelchairs cluttered the parking lot all the way up the ambulance ramp. He knew the ER staff was familiar with evacuation drills and it was evident in the calm, efficient way they performed their duties.

Alex would be busy but he hoped to catch even a glimpse of her. It was impossible to find anyone in the clutter of stretchers and wheelchairs. He scanned everyone in baggy blue scrubs. The hospital staff he noticed were either too tall, too wide, or too blond to be Alex.

Captain Smith announced that they would remain on standby. He suggested the men see if they could be of any help. Mike was the first one off the truck. He spotted Ralphie. Maybe he knew where Alex was. He hurried toward the paramedic.

"Hey, Ralphie, have you seen Alex?"

"Hi, Simone. She was just with me a few minutes ago. I think she's over there with Dr. Pratt." Ralphie pointed in the direction he had last seen Alex.

Mike couldn't help but wonder what Josh Pratt was doing here. Wasn't he some kind of fancy surgeon? The old lady in his care waved frantically. "Fireman, fireman, over here. You're just in time." The lady gasped between each word.

"Yes, ma'am. Everything is under control."

"No, listen to me. It's all my fault. She went back inside to get my . . ." The old lady coughed and smacked Josh on his arm. "You tell him. She was your wife, and you let her go."

"Alex just went to get something in the ER. She'll be right back," Josh said.

Mike wanted to grab Josh by the nonexistent collar

of his scrubs. How he could have allowed her to do something so stupid? Mike turned and ran back to his rig. He grabbed his air pack and shouted to Danny. "I'm going into the ER. Alex is inside."

"Let's go." Danny didn't waste time asking for details. He was right behind Mike when he pushed open the automatic doors.

Light smoke filled the corridor. Mike had been in far worse situations and decided he didn't need his mask just yet. The deeper he went into the ER, the smoke thickened. He didn't want to use up his air. Alex might need it when he found her. Damn that woman! Considering she was the daughter of a fire captain, this was a really dumb move. What was so important that she had to run back inside?

"What's she doing in here?" Danny shouted over the shrill of the fire alarm.

"Some old lady told me she came back to get a purse."

"I don't see anyone. Are you sure the old lady was with it?"

"A doctor confirmed the story." Mike didn't have time to explain that the doctor was Alex's ex-husband and a real jerk. "Remember she's a little bit of a thing. She won't be so easy to spot in the shadows."

Not much time had passed but Mike's eyes were beginning to burn. He blinked and through the smoke he saw a figure moving on her hands and knees along the wall. At least she had the sense to stay low.

"I see her!" He shouted to Danny and proceeded

forward. When he was in reach he turned on his flashlight and offered her his hand. "Alex, stay down and cover your mouth and nose with your shirt."

Alex's fingers reached out and locked around his. "Simone? Is that you?" She gasped, then coughed.

Her eyes burned and she couldn't see clearly but she heard Mike release a sigh. It was a good sign that she recognized him.

"Here, take a blow."

She removed the towel she had placed over her mouth. Desperate for a breath of clean air, she grabbed his mask and inhaled deeply. Sadie's bag slipped off her shoulder. The sharp shrill of the fire alarms screamed at her, reminding her how ridiculous her plan to rescue the lady's purse must seem to the sensible man in front of her.

Mike was on his knees beside her. "I'm going to get you out of here. Danny is waiting by the door."

"You're not going to throw me over your shoulder or anything like that?" She mumbled into the wet cloth.

"The idea had crossed my mind. Can you walk?"

She nodded but doubted he could see her gesture through the smoke. She reached up and tightened her hold on his hand.

Mike pointed to the large black leather bag tucked under her arm. He reached over to take it. "Leave the bag here."

She vehemently shook her head, doubting he could see the gesture through the smoke. In a hoarse voice she said, "I can't." Silly as it was, she couldn't abandon her quest now. Not after risking her life and the life of this brave man.

Arguing would just waste time. Mike led the way toward the door.

By the time they reached the fresh air, word of Alex's predicament had spread. Her co-workers were waiting with a stretcher and oxygen.

"Give her some oxygen STAT and get their eyes washed," someone ordered.

Alex coughed, and Mike felt her legs give way. Instinct dictated his next move. Without hesitating he scooped her in his arms and carried her to the waiting stretcher. She felt so light but even through his heavy rubber coat he liked the feel of her clinging to him.

She offered little resistance when one of the ER physicians placed a lighted probe on the surface of her finger. He stayed by her side until he was sure the sensor registered an oxygen saturation in an acceptable range.

Someone in pink scrubs handed Mike water. He took a sip but couldn't swallow. He turned and spit it out.

Alex reached for him. "Are you okay?"

"Fine."

A nurse tapped Mike on the shoulder and pointed to his eyes. He knew he needed them washed but didn't want to walk away from Alex. He squatted next to the stretcher and allowed the nurse to do her job. When she was done he stood up, faced Alex, and asked, "What was so important that you had to go back inside?"

"Mrs. Bell left her pocketbook." Alex handed the overstuffed bag to one of the nurses. "Give this to Sadie."

"Makes no sense to me." Mike wiped the back of his hand across his nose and sniffed.

"Exactly what I told her before she ran into the building." Josh stood on the opposite side of the stretcher. "Thank goodness you're okay."

Mike cringed when Josh took Alex's hand. He remembered how gentle her fingers felt when she reached out to grab onto him.

Alex slipped her hand away from Josh and reached up to flatten the corduroy collar on Mike's rubber coat. "You still hold to your rule, only one rescue per lady in distress?" she asked. "Looks like I've filled my quota for the year."

"Just for the month. Tomorrow starts a new month. Let's see what that brings."

"Okay, guys. She needs some blood tests." A doctor in a white lab coat pushed his way through.

Mike read the name on the badge, Dr. James Frank, ER Director. He could tell by the look on the doctor's face that he, too, was clearly upset by Alex's action. Confident that Alex was in the best care, Mike stepped back.

"Really, I'm fine. There's no need to do any tests." She tried to lift herself up on her elbows.

"Alex, I can't believe you did such a stupid thing. Now you have to pay the price. You know these tests are necessary for anybody we suspect has suffered from smoke inhalation." The doctor felt for a pulse in her wrist. "I'm going to do a blood gas. I'll try to draw enough blood for a carboxyhemoglobin level. We have to be sure there's no chance of carbon monoxide intoxication."

Alex winced when the needle pierced her skin. Mike desperately wanted to stand beside her and offer some comfort but her colleagues had formed a protective circle around her.

Mike decided to check back with his captain. On the other side of the building, firefighters zapped of energy sat on the back of their trucks. Mike recognized their looks of satisfaction. The fire had been put out. The smoke turned from gray to white. There was no reason for his engine company to stay around.

He rushed back to see Alex before he left. He thought she looked a little gray and then noticed the emesis basin in her lap.

"What happened?" he asked the nurse to his right.

"You missed it. Poor Alex. She sat up too fast and couldn't reach the emesis basin in time." The nurse bit her lip to hide her smile. "Dr. Pratt was directly in the line of fire."

Mike saw the wet mess on Josh's surgical scrubs and the equally sour expression on his face. He noticed how most of the staff around Alex tried to hide their snickers and smiles.

The incident sent Josh into a frenzy, and he rushed back to his clinic to change. Mike felt better about leaving now that Josh was gone too.

Alex still looked a little pale when Mike approached the stretcher. "You listen to the doctor and stay out of burning buildings," he said.

"I'll try."

"I guess you didn't read your horoscope this morning." Now that the danger had passed Mike tried to lighten up the tension.

"I was too busy. I didn't get a chance. You wouldn't happen to know what it said?"

"If I remember correctly . . ." Mike pretended to think for a moment. "You're a Scorpio?"

"That's right."

"Let's see. I think it read something like this: life can be perilous. Don't retrace your steps." He studied her. He could tell he had her attention. "And, it also said, 'you should open your mind to amorous adventure.' "

"Did it really?" A faint sparkle twinkled in her reddened eyes. The color was returning to her cheeks.

He realized she could easily check the newspaper. "The first part is yours. The part about amorous adventure is mine."

"You checked your star sign?"

"Didn't you hear? They added asparagus to the charts."

He liked the way the corners of her eyes wrinkled when she laughed. He wanted to stay with her and make her smile all day.

Captain Smith came up behind him. "Time to go, Simone. This the little lady you rushed in to save?"

"Yes, sir." Mike held his breath. The captain knew about his bet with the guys. He hoped he wasn't about to let it slip.

"You know what they say about this guy? Smarts,

guts, and just a little bit crazy." The captain put his arm around Mike's shoulder. "Don't let his tough guy exterior fool ya. Inside he's got a heart of chocolate mush. But he loves a good challenge. So you give him a run for his money."

"I'll have to remember that," Alex said.

Mike wondered if she would try to decipher the meaning of the captain's word? She was, after all, the daughter of a fire captain and knew all about firehouse humor. He could only hope she was too exhausted and would shrug off his captain's remark.

Mike had only taken a few steps when he heard his name. He turned.

"Hey, Simone." Alex's voice was a hoarse whisper. "Stay safe."

The words held their own meaning, but the concern in her expression would stay with him for a while.

Chapter Six

*Horoscope: Take time to know a man
and he could be the love of your life.*

Alex sat in the passenger seat of Chloe's red VW Bug and stared at the funky color of her spiked hair.

"Mosh Orange. In honor of Halloween," Chloe offered as an explanation.

"Very becoming. I like it better than the electric purple." Alex leaned back and watched the traffic light change from red to green.

Chloe never failed to add humor to her life. Today, however, she turned out to be a real life saver. Alex had planned to take the bus home once she was released. Dr. Frank laughed and refused to discharge her from the ER unless she had a ride home. She tried to compromise and suggested she would call a cab. Dr. Frank knew her too well. He wouldn't release her unless he had a guarantee someone would deliver her beyond her front door.

He forced her to admit that she hadn't been thinking clearly when she ran back into the smoky ER, and convinced her to call Chloe. Chloe was a good choice. Josh would have probably annoyed her with a thousand and one excuses why he couldn't pick her up, and she was not in the mood to hear her brothers rant on and on about her stupid action.

"Poor thing. How are you feeling?" Chloe asked as she pulled up in front of the new gourmet deli on Smith Street.

"I'm fine, really." She knew her voice sounded tired.

"After some of Al's tortilla chicken soup you'll feel like new." Chloe offered her hand and helped Alex from the car.

The warm breezes from the afternoon had turned to an autumn chill. With all of today's excitement, Alex had forgotten that it was Halloween. A group of kids dressed in scary alien costumes raced by. She remembered the neighborhood merchants participated in a program that encouraged trick or treaters to visit crowded areas.

She looked at Chloe and asked, "Who's minding the store?"

"Don't worry. Max is there."

Alex wasn't surprised. She knew it would be impossible to keep her grandfather away on Halloween. He loved the idea that everyone dressed in ridiculous costumes just to get their hands on some chocolate.

Just outside the deli they ran into Chloe's Aunt Bessie. The eccentric lady looked like an aged version of the young girl. Chloe lived with her aunt in the apartment building the elderly woman owned on Butler Street. Chloe was very fond of her aunt and credited her with instilling in her a love for experimenting with cocoa. People in the neighborhood often commented on how the walls of Bessie's building smelled like they were made of chocolate and were not surprised that her niece had inherited her talent.

"You poor child. Chloe called and told me how you ran into a burning building to save an old lady." A big smile crossed her face, making her eyelids disappear in a line of wrinkles. "She also told me how that handsome firefighter carried you out in his arms."

"Bessie, I think the story is a little twisted. I went in to get a purse for one of my patients. There were no flames and the firemen who helped me were just doing their jobs."

"Okay, dear. Whatever you say." Bessie winked at Chloe. "You take good care of her. She's a dear friend." Arthritic fingers took Alex's hand and squeezed the best they could. "Good-bye girls. Happy Halloween." Bessie chuckled as she pulled her shopping cart down the street.

Inside the deli the line at the take-out counter snaked through the store. Alex thought about how nobody cooked anymore; everyone ate on the run.

Chloe pulled a ticket from the red number machine. "We've got sixty-seven."

Alex glanced at the neon number over the counter. It

flashed the number sixty. The countermen moved swiftly, slicing and wrapping each order.

"We shouldn't have to wait too long," she said.

"Good. You can tell me again how that wonderful man ran into the burning building to save you." Chloe didn't wait for her response; she continued with her own version of the story. "You were confused, lost in the smoke." Her eyes widened with astonishment. "And through the flames you saw him. That wonderful man. He reached for you and . . ." Chloe inhaled and clasped her hands to her chest. "Did he throw you over his shoulder and carry you out of the building?"

Alex knew she had to stop Chloe from spinning the tall tale any further. Her story would flow from the lips of not only Aunt Bessie but everyone that entered the chocolate shop. Alex had to put a stop to it immediately.

"Chloe, stop, now."

"I'm sorry." She gave her an apologetic shrug. "I love the drama." She took Alex's hands. "Please tell me the story one more time."

"I should have never gone back inside." Repeating over and over again the story of her foolish action only accentuated the annoyance she felt with herself. "There were no flames, just smoke. I lost my sense of direction for a few seconds. That's it. Nothing else." She released a long slow breath. "Now tell me, how are the truffles selling?"

"You're just changing the subject so we don't talk about him. Admit it. He's a nice guy, and you're attracted to him."

Chloe leaned forward and lowered her voice. "And he's got great quads."

"Number sixty-seven," the counterman called.

Alex breathed a sigh of relief as Chloe walked away. She wanted to believe that the powerful feelings that surfaced each time she retold the story had nothing to do with the man who had come to her rescue. She couldn't forget the comfort and security she felt when she realized the hand she had reached out to clutch belonged to Mike Simone. She could still remember her knees turning to pudding and how she found security against the solid curve of his body. And how he lifted her in his strong arms and placed her gently on the stretcher, all the time thinking of her before his own discomfort. No one had ever done that before. It had been an emotionally charged day. She would need to get her feelings in check before she returned home and her grandfather started asking questions.

Chloe waved to her from the counter.

Stiff and sore from the hours she had spent lying on an ER stretcher, Alex searched for a place where she would be away from the crowd. She was just about to tell Chloe she would wait in the car when she heard her name.

"Alex?"

She turned to look behind her.

Mike Simone, followed by his partner Danny, entered the store. Danny walked off toward the deli counter while Mike headed straight toward her.

"How are you?" He looked her over from the top of

her disheveled hair to the dusty toes of her clogs. Perhaps he was reassuring himself that the smoke had left no ill effects.

She forced a tired smile, hoping to look somewhat presentable. She must have looked awful after being in the ER for so many hours. "I'm fine." She tried to sound convincing. Her eyes still burned and every muscle in her body ached.

"Getting something for dinner?" He nodded in the direction of the enticing aromas seeping over the counter.

"Chloe insisted I needed some chicken soup."

"No chocolate?" Mike inched closer, allowing a man with several packages to pass.

"Women can't live by chocolate alone. We do need something more substantial." She glanced down and noticed his heavy black shoes. Instinctively her eyes traveled up the length of his well-toned body. She stopped at the hooks of his suspenders and felt heat color her cheeks. "I know we sometimes obsess over it." My god, why was she blabbing like this? "Chocolate—I'm talking about chocolate." She felt the need to clarify her obsession.

"Chocolate is great. I've been known to stuff myself on occasion. What else is it you need?" A provocative smile curled his lips.

"I need . . ." Her eyes studied his face. What a great face. She looked away and nodded in the direction of the counter. "A hot bath and Al's tortilla chicken soup."

They both laughed at her answer, and she quickly forgot her embarrassment. What was it about Mike that made her feel so comfortable? She didn't try to think ahead before she said something like she so often had done when she spoke to Josh.

"What about you? If you're picking up dinner, you should try the soup," she suggested.

"I already ate. Danny and I are shopping for the fire-house. I have kitchen duty at the end of the week. We're here to get some sausage for my sauce."

"What, no chocolate cake?"

"Not until it's perfected. I'm working on it."

The tenderness and sincerity of his smile dazzled her. She tried to picture this hunk of a man standing over a hot stove stirring a huge pot of sauce. Surprisingly, the image was very pleasant. She was beginning to believe there wasn't anything he couldn't do.

"There you are." Danny, Mike's partner, came rushing toward them. "Look who I found." He was almost dragging Nilda, the astrologer, behind him. When he noticed Alex, he stopped abruptly.

"Hey, little lady, how are ya?" He looked from Alex to Mike with a suspicious glance.

"I'm fine, thanks to the two of you," Alex said.

"You should take it easy for a few days. Don't rush back to work." Danny looked at Mike for confirmation. "Don't ya think she should take off a few days?"

Mike looked startled by Danny and Nilda's sudden appearance. "Sure, she should take it easy." He began edging his way toward the meat counter, encouraging Danny and Nilda to follow.

Mike was acting odd all of a sudden. And why was

Danny so eager to bring Nilda over to Mike? There was an awkward silence until Nilda spoke.

"Poor dear, was there any warning in your sun forecast?" Nilda asked.

"I didn't get a chance to check today," Alex said.

"Those forecasts in the daily paper can be very general. Now, if someone was really interested . . ." Nilda turned toward Mike. "A reputable astrologer would look at more than a sun sign. When I do a chart I look at the planets and the elements in relation to the sun."

Why was Nilda lecturing Mr. Asparagus on sun charts? Mike seemed to be holding his breath. Was that a hostile glare he gave his partner? Alex had never seen him look so tense.

"Nilda," Danny interrupted. "Didn't you want to ask Mike about your new space heater? Maybe he can stop by and check it out."

"Yes, yes, my space heater. Stop by tomorrow evening. I should have everything . . . ah . . . my heater set up by then."

Nilda turned to leave and almost ran into Chloe, her arms full of plastic grocery bags.

"I thought you were just going to buy soup." Alex reached over and took some of the packages from Chloe.

"Maybe you'll be hungry. I just bought a little tabouli, bean salad, and . . ." Chloe noticed Mike and Danny. She shoved her bags into Alex's arms. With both hands she reached out to clasp Mike in a firm handshake. "Thank you. Thank you for saving my poor baby from that blazing inferno."

"Chloe!" Alex scolded. Embarrassed by her burst of melodrama, Alex wanted to get Chloe away before she got out of control. Alex shifted the weight of the bags into the nook of her elbow. Why did the packers insist on putting each item in its own bag? With her free hand, she grabbed Chloe by the arm. Chloe struggled to stay, but Alex was determined and guided her away. "These men have shopping to do."

Over her shoulder Chloe called back to Mike, "When's the bake-off?"

"In a couple of weeks," Mike said.

"Stop by tomorrow. Maybe I can help you with that chocolate frosting."

"Chloe," Alex gasped. She leaned close and whispered, "You know you can't give him the recipe."

"Maybe with my guidance he'll discover what's missing on his own." Chloe looked at her with an expression of wide-eyed innocence. "We owe him something for saving your life."

"I wouldn't exactly call it saving my life, but he has come to my rescue twice in the last forty-eight hours." As much as she liked the idea of Mike hanging around the shop she knew this was dangerous territory. She reached for Chloe's arm and conceded. "Okay, but remember he has to find the blend on his own." Tightening her grip, she added, "Make sure Grandpa Max is not going to show up."

Mike watched Alex drag poor Chloe away. Outside he caught her glancing through the window. He smiled as she attempted to confine her unruly curls. Her hair had the kind of mussed look you have when you first get out of bed. He would bet she looked great in the morning.

Even without the invitation from Chloe, Mike had every intention of stopping by the chocolate shop real soon. Tomorrow, November first, whether he liked it or not, the horoscope challenge would officially begin. He turned toward the meat counter and took the sample of luganega the butcher handed him. The spicy sausage stuck in his throat. He coughed, attempting to clear his throat.

Danny came over and patted him on the back. "Go down the wrong way?"

"I'm okay." Mike cleared his throat. "I don't like where this whole thing is going. What were you thinking, bringing Nilda over while I was talking to Alex?"

"Getting cold feet? I thought you could use some help from an expert." Danny reached for a sample from the counter. He popped a piece of turkey sausage into his mouth.

"I don't like where this whole bet thing is going. I don't want to start a relationship based on deception."

Danny threw back his head and laughed. "You're much too honest, kid. Women like a little foreplay."

"If that's your idea of foreplay, your wife's in trouble." Mike laughed too, releasing some of the tension that had suddenly surfaced. He realized if he was going to get through the month he would have to look at the light side of this ridiculous challenge.

"Ya got nothing to worry about. Alex believed that

nonsense about a heater." Danny wiggled his eyebrows. "Did you like how I came up with that story? If you ask Nilda for help, Alex will never suspect a thing."

"I hope you're right." Somehow the idea of the bet and using Alex's star chart didn't sit right.

"How about we sweeten the bet with a little cash?" Danny became serious. "We all remember what happened to your first partner and how the burn center helped get him back on his feet. I'm sure I can get the guys to pass around a helmet and help increase your donation."

"What do you have in mind?"

"What if the guys agree to drop some spare change in the hat every day that you follow Alex's horoscope?"

Mike cleared his throat. "If all the money goes to the burn center, you're making it hard for me to refuse."

"All you have to do is keep your end of the agreement. You follow her chart, and we'll add to the pot." Danny had more than sweetened the bet. He had hit on a charity very close to Mike's heart. When he was a rookie, Mike witnessed a terrible accident at a tenement fire. His partner fell through the floor and spent months being treated in the burn unit at County. It was a miracle the man survived.

Mike weighed his options. Going back on the bet was not a choice. The guys would never let him live it down. How had his intentions gotten so out of hand? All he wanted was to ask Alex out. Okay maybe asking out the daughter of a retired fire captain had some kinks. Who was he kidding? There was one very big glitch and it had nothing to do with Alex's father being retired from the job. It was the old man, Max Martinelli. Max treated him like he was the descendant of some dreadful untouchable. If he raised extra money for the burn center and got closer to Alex at the same time, all the aggravation would be worth Max's scorn.

"All right," he said. "I'll forget you almost blew the whole thing by bringing Nilda over. Just remember that you promised not to tell anyone else in the neighborhood."

"Whatever you say." Danny grinned. "Why don't you see what her horoscope says for today? Poor girl looks like she could use a special treat." He slapped Mike on the back. "Maybe a slice of your cake or something like that."

Mike thought about what Danny said. Had he passed up the perfect opportunity to ask Alex out? He could have invited her out for coffee or pizza. No, too cliché. Hot chocolate would work. There was nothing threatening about drinking a cup of hot chocolate.

She wouldn't be able to refuse such an invitation. After all, he had saved her from a burning building. But what if she accepted his invitation purely out of a sense of obligation? Guys who worked for the department a long time often told stories of reactions of people overwhelmed with gratitude. He wouldn't want Alex to be obligated to him. That was the least of his problems.

There was the old man. He imagined Max Martinelli might be less than congenial if he knew the truth about Mike's intentions. But he wanted to date his granddaughter more than he wanted to find the missing ingredient in his frosting. Putting aside Danny's offer to sweeten the donation to the burn unit, Mike would still rather be with Alex than win the bet. Would he have to sacrifice one for the other? Maybe he could have both. After all, accepting Chloe's offer would only bring him closer to Alex.

Let the guys at the house believe what they wanted. Mike knew the connection between him and Alex had nothing to do with the stars and planets. It was the chocolate that would bring them together.

Chapter Seven

Horoscope reading: Let the new moon allow you to start fresh. Open your heart to someone with whom you share a common bond.

Alex stared at her drooping eyelids. The bright bathroom lights only enhanced her tired image. As a result of the endless hours she spent fighting with her pillow, she now felt like she had a hangover. Having the next few days off to rest turned out to be a blessing. She suspected her restless night's sleep was a result of her experiences the previous day. She would like to blame the smoke she inhaled, but she knew that her thoughts about her rescuer were responsible for her twisting and turning. In such a short time Mike Simone had somehow found his way into her already complicated life.

Two disasters in less then one week must definitely

be her quota: first the fire at the fair and then the fire in the ER. What were the odds that another unpleasant event would bring them together again? She assumed the chances were slim.

Why did it have to be another grim event? What if something pleasant brought them together?

As hard as she tried she couldn't shake the memory of being cradled in Mike's arms, so male, so secure. She couldn't deny the mutual temptation. But, no, no, no, she refused to go back on her vow. She would never date a firefighter. Not after bearing witness to her father's debilitating illness that resulted from the hazards of the job.

Even more convincing was the strange aversion her grandfather had toward the Simone family. She couldn't hurt that sweet old man by dating a Simone. As much as there was some strange catalyst throwing her and Mike together, there were equal opposing forces pulling them apart.

When she did run into Mike again she would just have to suppress her attraction to him. She would turn on the ladylike reserve—let him think she's cold and aloof. It might be just the trick to discourage any romantic thoughts he might be considering.

She sighed and shook her head. "Foolish girl," she said to the sorry-looking image in the mirror.

The best thing she could do today was to find some way to occupy both her thoughts and her time. One thing was for certain, she had no intention of wasting the day lying idle in bed. She looked back at the mirror, catching a glimpse of her red eyes, a constant reminder of her foolish action. She reached for the saline eye drops, squeezed a drop in each eye, then blinked rapidly, trying to clear the haze and vanish the image of Mike in his bunker gear.

Anxious to get out of the house, she dressed quickly and raced down the stairs. She stopped at the kitchen table. Her grandfather, always thoughtful, had folded the morning paper into neat little rectangles so that her horoscope lay there ready to be read. She tossed it into her pocketbook and rushed out the front door. The chocolate shop would be just the place for her to stay busy today.

When she entered the shop, Chloe was already busy packaging delicate homemade marshmallows into crinkly little bags. She placed several hand cut squares in each bag and twisted shiny gold ties around the ends. Alex thought it was a perfectly mindless task. Just what the doctor ordered.

Chloe gratefully handed the bags to Alex. "Place ten pink and five white marshmallows in each bag." She watched Alex pack a bag. Satisfied that she was up to the task, Chloe vanished to the back of the store.

Alex must have packaged thousands of candies before someone finally entered the store. She suspected everyone was still on a sugar high from Halloween night. When the door opened, a chilly November wind swirled through the empty space between the counters. Nilda, the astrologer, blew in.

"It feels like it turned cold overnight." The older woman forced the door shut behind her.

"Winter will be here before you know it," Alex said. "It's good that you're having your heater checked today."

"My heater." Nilda stared at her with a blank look.

Alex was concerned by the older woman's response. Nilda had a razor sharp mind. Forgetting such a recent conversation seemed very odd. "Don't you remember? You asked one of the firemen, Mike, to check it out."

"Yes, yes, that handsome young man. He's stopping by my store later." Nilda nodded.

"Oh, the heater is for your store. I thought it was for your apartment." Alex was getting confused and decided to drop the subject.

"Who's stopping where?" Chloe joined them.

"We were just talking about the sudden change in the weather." The last thing Alex wanted was to have Chloe bring up Mike Simone in front of Nilda.

No such luck. Chloe regarded the ladies with interest. "What's the weather have to do with someone visiting Nilda? Someone we know searching for their spiritual identity?"

It bothered Alex when Chloe made fun of her daily predictions. Was she baiting her now? Had she heard Nilda mention Mike?

Nilda stepped away. She glanced over the counter and through the opened back door. "Is your grandfather here today?"

"No, he had a doctor's appointment."

"I hope he's feeling better." Nilda turned her attention back to the chocolates in the display case.

Chloe followed her. She reached into the candy case, removed two truffles, and placed them on the scale. She handed one truffle to Nilda and the other she carefully wrapped in paper and placed in a small white bag. "What's going on tonight?" she leaned over the counter and whispered.

"I'm having my heater inspected by one of the boys from the firehouse."

"Not the good-looking one who saved Alex from the towering inferno."

"Chloe, you have got to stop," Alex chided.

"I was going to suggest, if Nilda didn't want to be alone with a strange man, we could stop by."

"She doesn't need anyone there watching Mike inspect her heater."

"It wouldn't be the heater we'd be watching," Chloe suggested.

"Chloe." This time there was no mistaking the warning in Alex's voice.

"Don't worry. I won't be alone. Nathan is working today." Nilda reached for her candy.

"The high Wicca priest?" Chloe snickered.

Alex's dark eyes reprimanded Chloe. She turned to Nilda, attempting to soften Chloe's sarcasm, and once again changed the subject. "Mike will be in and out quickly. He'll probably just verify that you set up the heater according to the manufacturer's instructions and suggest you get a CO detector."

Chloe turned to Nilda, who seemed to have a blank

look on her face. "I bet Mike would find our Alex irresistible if he heard her talking like that. Heaters and detectors . . . Ow!" Chloe shook off an imaginary shiver.

Alex stepped behind the counter and nudged Chloe away with her hip. "Isn't there something you have to do?"

"No." Chloe stepped aside and let Alex ring up Nilda's purchase. She glanced at the astrologer and suggested, "Maybe you can sell that hunk some special oils or one of those dream-analysis books."

Alex answered, "I doubt Mike Simone is interested in having his dreams picked apart." She hesitated for a moment before closing the drawer of the cash register. Mike was most likely coming off of a forty-eight-hour shift. If he had any time to sleep last night, did she come into his dreams the way he had hers?

"Alex is right." Nilda's forced laugh caught Alex's attention. "He doesn't believe in cosmic forces or that the placement of the sun at your birth has anything to do with who or what you are."

"He told you all this recently?" Alex was curious to find out when Nilda had such an involved conversation about the elements with Mr. Asparagus.

"You remember. I had that little candle fire. Those boys saved my store." Nilda reached for her change. "I stop by the firehouse with treats every so often." She opened her pocketbook, tossed in her change, and said, "Oh, by the way I brought you your new chart for November."

Alex didn't remember asking for a sun chart for the

new month. She usually stopped by Nilda's store when she wanted a chart.

Nilda noticed her surprise. "It's an early birthday present."

Alex accepted the stack of computer printouts. "Anything going to shock me?"

"It does forecast some heat in your love life." The playful gleam in Nilda's eyes suggested more than just heat.

Knowing her forecast in advance wasn't such a bad idea. The way October had ended, a little forewarning might be exactly what she needed to prevent exposure to future disasters.

She took a quick glance at her chart. She couldn't resist reading out loud the first line of her romanticscope. "The new month shows you opening your heart to someone with whom you have a common bond."

Nilda gave her a curious glance. "Well. What do you think?"

"Interesting." Alex tried to sound matter-of-fact.

"Oh no, I think it's more than interesting." Chloe was reading over her shoulder. "Let me see." She positioned her hands palms up as if they were a scale trying to balance heavy objects. "Is the common bond with someone you have a connected past? Oops." She tipped her right hand lower than the left. "Or is it someone with a common link . . ."—her entire body leaned in the opposite direction and there was a big smile on her face when she said—". . . to the fire department."

"You know one forecast doesn't stand alone." Alex looked from Chloe to Nilda. Was Nilda smiling at

Chloe's silly antics? "I'll have to read on and see how Nilda combined all the elements."

"Even though I don't believe in all this stuff, I'm glad I'll be around to see how it turns out." Chloe excused herself.

"She can be a handful sometimes." Alex watched Chloe disappear into the back of the store. "But you gotta love her."

"Anyone who can make chocolate like this is wonderful." Nilda bit into her truffle. "Say hello to Max," she said on her way out.

Alex sat on a stool behind the counter and skimmed the pages of her chart. Nilda had covered all the elements as well as her health and financial forecasts. Alex didn't pay much attention to the last two and turned back to her romantic chart. The words *common bond* jumped at her.

She dared to imagine the bond could be with Josh. Only by some calamitous alignment of the planets could she ever imagine getting back together with that pompous jerk. She reached into the display case and popped a truffle in her mouth. The luscious filling altered the bad taste thoughts of Josh left her with.

Alex smiled. That sinfully sexy firefighter was another possibility. As pleasant as the thought was, it would never happen. Not as long as his name was Simone.

The front door bell announced the arrival of another customer. Alex looked up and found herself looking directly at Mike Simone. What would he say if knew where her thoughts had just been? She paled at the possibility.

"Hi. Are you feeling okay? You look a little pale." The concern in his voice touched her.

"I'm fine," she lied. Sure, physically she felt fine. But mentally she couldn't shake the awkward feeling that lingered about her bumbling decision to retrieve Sadie's pocketbook. She stood up and walked around the counter. Unsure of what she should say next, she asked, "What brings you here this morning?"

"Did you forget?" He looked concerned. "Chloe offered to help with my frosting and . . ." He pulled an autumn bouquet overflowing with chrysanthemums from his shopping bag. "These are for you. I thought you might be here. You're not the type to stay home and nurse your wounds."

Alex glanced into the bag. It was filled with baking utensils and cake pans. He was really serious about this frosting thing. She accepted the flowers and studied him. What kind of man rescued you from a smoky corridor and then brought you flowers? Maybe it was just a gesture of good will for not making waves when Chloe offered to help him.

"Thanks for the flowers. I'll tell Chloe you're here." Alex had to walk away because Mike's every gesture reminded her of his sexual attractiveness. An attraction complemented by his kindness that she was finding difficult to ignore.

Chloe wasted no time in dragging her rookie chef back to the work counter.

Alex turned her attention to a sudden rush of customers. They kept her busy in the front of the store, forcing her to resist the urge to sneak peeks at Mike while he worked.

Busy weighing and wrapping assorted chocolate purchases, Alex didn't notice her friend, Sarah, come into the shop. Her accounting firm had an office nearby on Court Street.

"Well, my friend." Sarah approached the counter. "I'm glad to see you survived your little near-death encounter without any noticeable injuries." Sarah, an independent earth sign, was a contrast to Alex's water sign. She came behind the counter and reached into the display case for a sample.

Alex closed the cash register drawer and turned to her. "I'm sure you heard all about my experience, so I don't have to tell it again?"

Sarah nodded. She had a lot of clients in the neighborhood. Alex believed most of Sarah's clients were only too eager to share her horrid story with their accountant.

"You know how it goes, once someone on this block gets hold of a story . . ." She popped the chocolate in her mouth. "I heard the fireman who pulled you out is a real looker."

"Shh." Alex put her finger to her lip. "He's here now."

"What's he doing here?" Sarah turned in a circle looking for Mike. "Where is he?"

"In the back." Alex guided her close enough to the back room for Sarah to get a glimpse of Mike and Chloe.

They were so engrossed in their task, they didn't notice the snooping women. Chloe, with her usual gusto and passion, was demonstrating the art of blending chocolate. Alex hoped her enthusiasm wouldn't cause her to lower her guard and divulge any of Grandpa Max's secrets.

"That is one decadently delicious man. He can throw me over his shoulder and carry me to oblivion any day."

"You're as bad as Chloe. No one carried me over their shoulder. He just did his job. He guided me out of a smoky corridor."

"Sure you were probably delirious and don't remember anything."

"I was perfectly aware of everything." Her mind burned with the memory of every move and gesture Mike had made toward her. She tried to keep the memories pure and innocent, but enticing thoughts of his handsome face and strong arms filled her mind as she filled Sarah in on some of the details.

In spite of her wicked thoughts, she managed to say, "He was very concerned for my well-being once he got me to safety."

"Don't bore me with the details." Sarah yawned. She inched herself onto the stool behind the counter. "What's going on back there?"

"Chloe is helping him find the perfect frosting for his chocolate cake." Alex tried to sound matter-of-fact.

"That hunk of man bakes chocolate cakes?" Sarah asked then added, "Wow I'd go over my calorie count any day for a taste of something that good-looking."

Alex ignored her friend's comment on how appealing Mike looked. She already knew every inch of him that she could see by heart. Turning the subject back to his cake, she said, "He wants to enter the firefighters bake-off. If he wins the prize he plans to donate the money to the burn unit at County."

"Let's hope the panel of judges is all women. All he has to do is dazzle them with his looks, they won't care what the cake tastes like." Sarah glanced over her shoulder. "If he needs an accountant to help him disburse those funds, just send him my way."

"If he doesn't get the frosting right, there may not be any prize money to distribute."

"He's really serious about this chocolate business, isn't he?"

"Yes, very serious. The frosting has to complement the cake."

"Oh my God, Alex. Don't you see what this is all about?" Sarah clasped her chest with open palms. "This man is your destiny."

"Since when do you believe in destiny?"

"I don't, but this time it seems the heavens have made a match for you."

"You know I don't date firemen."

"It has nothing to do with your feelings over your dad's illness. It's very sad that he was forced to retire because of it, but . . ." Sarah reached over and pinched Alex's cheek. "Wake up and smell the frosting. It's all about the chocolate." Her friend's entire face spread into a smile. "I can't believe you don't see what's happening." Her eyes twinkled. "The chocolate brought you and this fireman together in the first place."

"You're crazy." Alex busied herself rearranging the trays in the case.

"Oh, am I?" Sarah jumped off the stool. "You're the one who believes the stars and planets affect your life. This is all within the realm of what you believe in. You and this firefighter cake baker belong together."

"How's that?"

"If you don't allow this to happen, you'll disturb the balance. You could end up dating the wrong guy for all the wrong reasons. You could take someone else's soul mate." Sarah looked at her with pleading eyes. "Just recap the events of the last couple of days."

Just a few hours ago Alex had thought about the fire at the fair and her stupid action in the ER. Both times Mike had come to the rescue. She thought she would never see him again. Could Sarah be right? Could chocolate be the common bond her horoscope predicted?

"Maybe you're right, but something between me and Mike can never happen." Alex picked up her horoscope. "Mike is a Simone. You know, one of those horrid people my grandfather always warned me to stay away from."

"He's a Simone?" Sarah swallowed hard and coughed.

Alex thought her friend was about to choke. She filled a glass with water and handed it to Sarah.

Regaining her composure, Sarah stood motionless for a second. When the look of horror left her face she managed to say, "You never said his name was Mike Simone?"

"You didn't ask."

"This might complicate the situation." Sarah looked to be in deep thought. "If he's related to that chocolate thief, Sal Simone, things could get sticky."

"Alex stared at Sarah, baffled. "I never said anything about chocolate thieves."

"Oh, come on. You know your grandfather has a decades-old quarrel with someone in the Simone family."

"I always knew about the feud but never understood what it was all about until recently. It was at the fair that I found out about the stolen chocolate recipe and Sal. How do you know about any of this?"

"I may be your best friend but I'm also Max's accountant. Some things are client/accountant confidentiality."

"I can understand why Chloe knew the story." Alex glanced at the chocolate-making artifacts hanging on the wall. "She believes even those old things have hidden chocolate secrets. It makes sense for her and my grandfather to shroud all their recipes in secrecy. But why would you know what happened? And why can't you tell me the rest of the story?"

Alex wanted to scream in frustration.

Chapter Eight

Horoscope reading: Your uncanny ability
will get you to the core of any issue.

The loud clatter of metal against tile distracted Sarah and Alex. In unison, they turned to see what had caused such a commotion.

Mike stepped through the door, followed by Chloe.

"Is everything okay?" Alex, caught off guard by the sight of Mike in a peppermint-stripe apron, bit her lip to hide her smile. The strings of the bib were tied behind his broad shoulders in a neat little bow. The serious expression on his face made her reconsider the possibility of finding humor in this situation.

Mike released the strings and handed the apron to Chloe. "I'm calling it quits for today."

Chloe hesitated before taking the apron. "Maybe if

we try a semisweet, the higher liquor content will make the chocolate flavor stronger."

"I don't have the time to fool around with the ingredients. The bake-off is in two weeks." Mike shrugged. "I'll just take my chances with what I've got." He didn't seem disturbed or angry, just resigned to the fact that his cake would have to be presented with the frosting he already had.

Alex watched Chloe, her body unusually tense, her frustration evident. Her pursed lips kept her from offering the one thing Mike needed. Alex understood, but neither she or Chloe had the right to give Mike what he needed, her grandfather's recipe.

Sarah always had an uncanny knack for sensing what her friend was feeling. She stepped from behind the counter, nudged Alex and whispered, "Remember your destiny."

Fate did not appear to be on her side at the moment. The chocolate, her common bond to Mike Simone, was about to separate them forever. If Mike walked out of the store, there was a good possibility she might never see him again.

Sarah, still standing behind Alex, once again echoed her feelings. This time her voice was much louder than a whisper. "Do something. You can't just let him walk away. You'll never know if he was the right one."

Mike stopped and turned. The corners of his lips curled in that little sly smile that made Alex's heart beat faster. Of course he had heard Sarah advertise her thoughts.

Alex felt her cheeks turn the color of the candy apples

in the store window. "What Sarah means is we'll never know if Mike's meant to win the cake bake-off."

"That's not what I was talking about and you know it," Sarah insisted.

It was time to say good-bye to her blabbermouth friend before Alex sunk deeper into a sticky mess. Grabbing Sarah by her shoulders, Alex ushered her toward the door. Not to be rude she glanced over her shoulder and made a hasty introduction. "This is Sarah. She was just leaving."

Alex turned and found Mike looking at her with more than a gleam of interest in his blue eyes. It was the kind of look that in another place and time would have swept her off her feet.

Mike stepped forward. "Destiny? Would that have anything to do with the compatibility of an asparagus and a Scorpio?"

She looked up at him. He was too good to be true. How did he always manage to say the right thing?

But Mike was no longer looking at her. His eyes darted past her toward the door, where something or someone had Sarah frozen in place.

Sarah turned on her heels and rushed into the store. "It's Max. He's coming up the street."

Quickly forgetting the moment she and Mike had just shared, Alex tensed with an awful feeling of apprehension.

Chloe reacted too. With her delicate artistic hands, she attempted to drag Mike out the back door. "Hurry, this way."

Mike's powerful body did not budge, prompting Sarah to grab his other arm. He stood steadfast while Chloe and Sarah tugged forward. They changed positions and tried to push the solid mass of muscle from behind, but Mike still did not budge. This was beginning to look like a scene out of *Keystone Cops.*

All this nonsense for a silly cake! Alex had to put a stop to the chaos before her grandfather walked in. Nervously she twisted a loose strand of hair. "Stop!" she shouted. "This is ridiculous. Let him go."

The girls released their hold. Mike stepped closer to Alex.

She was very aware of his physical closeness but did not move away. She thought she detected a flicker of amusement in Mike's eyes.

What could he find so amusing about this situation? There was nothing funny about what she and Chloe had taken the liberty of doing. How could she be so foolish, allowing Chloe to convince her to take part in this frosting caper? They had gone behind her grandfather's back and allowed a stranger—a very handsome stranger—to enter the secret chamber where Max's safely guarded recipes were prepared. And to add insult to injury, Mike was not just anyone, but a member of the dreaded Simone family.

"What's going on here?" Mike asked. "Your grandfather doesn't know I'm here? Does he?"

She shook her head and managed to mouth a soft "No." She should have known her grandfather would never stay away from the shop this time of year. And now they were all going to be caught with their hands in the mixing bowl.

"We'll just have to face him," she released a heavy sigh.

Off to her side, Chloe was nudging Sarah toward the back door.

Mike reached out and clasped their shoulders. "Where do you guys think you're going? You can't let Alex face the candymaker alone."

She was grateful for Mike's intervention. She wasn't prepared to take the brunt of Max's scorn by herself. Her thoughts, however, took on new meaning when Max entered the store. In an unsuccessful attempt to block his view, she stepped in front of her grandfather. Feeling like the monkey in the middle, she realized too late that that was a dumb move.

Max stared right past her. "What? What is he doing here?" He sputtered and turned as pale as a candy cane missing its stripes.

Mike offered Max his hand. "Nice to see you up and about."

"Hmph . . ." Max turned away.

Alex was not the only one holding her breath as they waited to see how Mike would react to Max's attack.

"Sorry to bother you, sir. I was just leaving." Mike turned toward the back of the store.

"You're going the wrong way, young man." With his good hand Max reached out and grabbed Mike by his shirt. He fingered a chocolate stain on the sleeve. "What's going on here?"

Mike offered no resistance when Sarah stepped in and offered a temporary solution. "I'll help Mike gather up his pots and pans, and we'll be on our way."

"Pots and pans? Has this man—a Simone—been near my special chocolate?" Max looked at Chloe, then Alex.

"It's not what you think, Grandpa."

"I'm not so old and feeble that I need you to tell me what I'm thinking." Max directed his next remark to Chloe. "I know what I see."

Chloe, in turn, looked to Alex for an intervention.

Alex threw her hands up in the air. Why did everyone always expect her to fix things? If she knew what everyone else seemed to know, the whole story of the connection between Grandpa's chocolate and the Simones, she might have been able to think of something useful to say, but she was clueless.

"Maybe everyone should leave." She regretted those words but couldn't think of an alternative solution. She signaled for Sarah to get Mike out of the store. She and Chloe would deal with her grandfather once Mike was out of the way. A quick glance at Chloe wringing her delicate hands, and Alex knew she would be on her own.

Max slammed the door with a bang and shouted, "Stay out and stay away from my granddaughter!" He stormed off in the direction of the candy kitchen.

Through the window, Alex watched Sarah link her arm in Mike's. Regardless of what had just happened, her friend would waste no time tossing her matchmaking skills into full swing. By the time they reached the corner, Mike Simone would have the opportunity to find out anything he ever wanted to know about Alex Martinelli.

Turning her attention back to the two sour balls in the store, Alex couldn't worry about what Sarah was telling Mike; she had bigger issues to deal with. Chloe and her grandfather walked out of the back room.

"He's all yours," Chloe whispered as she walked by.

Max waved his bandaged hand at Chloe. "How could you let that thieving Simone near my kitchen?"

"Mike has no interest in hearing about your silly feud." Chloe flung her hands hopelessly in the air. "And if he did, I doubt he would care about what happened. It was so long ago."

"What else are you hiding?" Alex asked.

"Now see what you've done!" Grandpa Max continued to shout at Chloe. "She didn't have to know, but I had to tell her because that boy showed up. You're right. It was a long time ago. Everything finally worked out. Until . . ." His voice cracked. "Until that Mike Simone showed up."

Alex felt it was unfair for Mike to be attacked when he wasn't there to defend himself. "Grandpa, Mike didn't just show up. He was doing his job and happened to be there when we needed him. Chloe and I felt the least we could do to show our gratitude was let him use our kitchen to work on his chocolate cake."

"Oh, you needed him here today?" Max retorted.

"Grandpa, you're not listening. I don't need Mike. I just felt obligated for everything he's done for us." She wasn't exactly lying. This wasn't the time or the place to admit she didn't need him, she wanted him.

"That's odd." Grandpa Max looked down at her with a forced smile. He could always tell when she wasn't being truthful. "Aren't you the one who explained his presence at the fair as always being on the job?" He raised a brow and asked, "Are you carrying on with that boy?"

"Of course not." Grandpa was right. Admitting to herself that she liked having Mike around was scary enough. The idea that she was attracted to a firefighter made it even more disconcerting. But what bothered her the most was her need to have Grandpa's approval before allowing this relationship to go any further.

"Young lady, I don't expect you to understand the connection between the Simones and my chocolate." Grandpa shot Chloe a wary look and pointed an accusing finger. "You should have known better."

"Maybe you should tell her why you feel the way you do," Chloe suggested before turning on her heels and disappearing into the back of the store.

"Grandpa, are you going to tell me the rest of the story?"

Max looked right at her and shook his head.

"You can think about it while I help Chloe clean up."

"Shouldn't take you long." Max reached for the newspaper Alex had been reading. "Wrap up that Simone junk and put it in its proper place—the Dumpster."

"Grandpa." Alex sighed. "The man is just trying to win the prize at the firefighters bake-off."

"Should have known there's money involved."

Alex listened to Max mumble to himself. No use trying to explain how Mike wanted to win for the honor of his firehouse and to help the burn center. Whatever her grandfather thought about the Simones he refused to believe Mike had another motive.

"I think it's time you told me everything that happened between you and Sal." She placed her hands on her hips. "I'm not moving until you tell me the reasons why you treat Mike the way you do."

Max looked at her out of the corner of his eye but didn't say anything.

"You are a stubborn old man." Alex had an idea that might appeal to Grandpa's sense of family. "Chloe knows. Sarah too. They're not even family."

"She tell you anything?"

"No. Sarah's a professional. She'd never breach her client's confidentiality."

"Smart girl. It wasn't for her to tell." A look of tired sadness passed over her grandfather's features. "Okay, you're right. You should know why I want you to stay away from that boy."

"But, Grandpa. How can you blame him for something that happened so long ago?"

"Shh." Max silenced her with a finger to his lip. "There's no doubt about it. He's a descendant of Sal's. Looks just like the man. Pleasant fellow, appealing to the ladies with his dark hair and blue eyes."

Alex suspected, although the man Grandpa described sounded just like Mike, he wasn't talking about her firefighter. She waited for Grandpa to continue.

.

"Sal was my partner in the chocolate business. We started making candy on my mother's kitchen table and sold it to the neighbors. They liked it, so we opened a shop on Hoyt Street."

Alex nodded. She had heard the story of how the Chocolate Boutique was started, minus any mention of a partner. "What happened to Sal?" she asked.

"He had grand ideas. Wanted to sail around the world."

"Did he? He left you with the store?"

"*Phh . . .*" Grandpa rolled his eyes. "He left all right. With our chocolate recipe."

"The same one you still use today?" Alex wished she had accepted her grandfather's offer to learn the business. Things would make more sense now.

"Whose story is this?" Grandpa gave her a sly look.

"Your story." If she wanted to hear the rest, she had better remain silent and let her grandfather finish what he had to say.

"He told me he had an offer from some big commercial candy manufacturer. I told him if we sold the recipe we'd have to start from scratch. He disagreed."

"Did he steal the recipe and sell it?" She couldn't contain her comments any longer.

"He didn't have to steal it. He knew the ingredients as well as I did. We lived and breathed every ingredient that went into those recipes." Grandpa opened a drawer behind the counter.

Patiently Alex watched and waited while he shuffled through some old register tapes, candy wrappers, and ribbons.

"Ahh, here it is." He removed his little black book of chocolate and opened it to a yellow-tinged page. "Just in case something happened to both of us, we wrote it down."

She took the book from Max and walked over to a table to study it. She held it up to the light hoping to illuminate the print. "How can you read this? So many of the words are faded."

Max pulled up a chair next to her. "I may forget a lot of things but not what's written on this page." He taped his head. "It's all up here."

Everyone knew about Grandpa's little black book but never paid much attention to its contents. She assumed it was just a memento of the past. Who would have thought the cause of the feud between the Simones and Martinellis was on this ancient piece of paper.

"When did you write in this book?"

"It was over fifty years ago." Grandpa took the book, tossed it back on the table.

"Did Sal sell the recipe for a lot of money?"

"It was a lot of money back then, but I wasn't interested. Even when I found out the candy company didn't want the chocolate recipe, only wanted our nugget filling, I refused to sell."

"Didn't he offer you a fair share of the money?"

"*Phh.* I told him to keep his sneaky money. Imagine making deals behind his partner's back?" Grandpa looked hurt. "We worked our fingers to the bone to open this place." He sank deeper into his chair. "We agreed to the entire partnership with just an honest man's handshake. Back then we didn't need all those sugar-coated contracts between friends." Grandpa shook his head in disgust. "The filling was replaceable."

But not their friendship. Some things began to make sense. Grandpa couldn't let the hurt go because he believed his best friend had deceived him. Would he have given the chocolate recipe to Sal if he hadn't made the deal behind his back? There was still more to the story, she sensed.

Max walked over to the candy counter. He studied his masterpieces for a moment and then picked out Alex's favorite, a sweet amaretto and marshmallow filling, covered with dark chocolate. He didn't offer it to her. He took a bite.

"A perfect blend. Chloe is a genius." After chewing for a moment he said, "Your grandmother, Gladys, would have liked this one too."

Alex blinked away a tear at Grandpa's mention of her grandmother. Talking about the past probably stirred memories of his late wife.

She understood why she had never been privy to the story. Of course Chloe needed to know, and that was why they shrouded every new product in such secrecy. But why did Sarah know about Sal? The incident happened way before she or her friend as born—decades ago, in another century.

"Grandpa, does Sal still own his share of the chocolate recipe?"

"Why wouldn't he? I'm not a snake like him. I still honor my end of our partnership."

Alex smiled, suddenly realizing how Sarah was involved. "And you still send him his share of the profits?"

"Ahh, rubbish." Grandpa gave her sideways glance. "I sense those wheels turning in your pretty head. What are you up to?"

"What if a descendant of Sal's made some modifications and used the chocolate to make a . . ."—she considered the best way to present her idea to him—"someone could use the original recipe and make a . . ."

The words came from behind. "A frosting." Chloe had been listening the whole time. She clapped her hands together. "I love it."

"Crazy youngsters," Max said. "You want me to just hand this recipe over to that firefighter?"

"Yes." Chloe and Alex said in unison.

"We've modified the recipe a little but our chocolate is not so far away from the original," Chloe explained. "We wouldn't be revealing all our secrets if Mike used a part of the original recipe in his frosting. The rules of the firefighters bake-off allow him to use an original or family recipe only." She clasped her hands and sighed. "What could be more perfect. It's a beautiful story, and Mike would be sure to win."

Alex bit her lip and waited for her grandfather to respond.

But Max was not so easy to convince. "For all you know that could have been that young man's plan all along."

"Grandpa, he didn't even know who you were when he helped you at the fair."

"He's a conniving Simone." Max looked over his shoulder and spit, just like he always did when he said the dreaded name. "I'm not giving him even a smidgen of my secret blend."

Maybe the day when she first met Mike she might have believed her grandfather's distrust, but not now. Mike was too devoted to the department to have acted out of his own interest.

"Grandpa, wouldn't it be nice to do something for a man who's always taking care of other people?"

Max gave her a crooked glance. "You think so? You take care of everyone. Who rewards you for what you do?"

She had never seen her grandfather so disagreeable. "People are always doing nice things for the nurses at County."

"Simones are not agreeable people. You're a big girl, I can't tell you what to do. If you're smart you'll stay away from that boy and his bad blood." Max kicked the shopping bag full of Mike's baking pans. "Get rid of this trash before I get back."

Chloe stood next to her and watched Max leave the store. "This is an ugly bag of gummy worms. We're going to need some reinforcements to get out of this predicament."

"Exactly what I've been thinking." Alex wasn't going to leave everyone in this mess, especially her grandfather. It bothered her to see him so disturbed. "We need someone who can not only help Mike win the bake-off but help Max heal his old wounds too." She reached for the phone.

"Who are you calling?" Chloe trotted behind her.

"Sarah." She gave Chloe a don't-stop-me-look.

"Weren't you paying attention? Didn't you hear Max yell at her too?" Chloe asked with growing anxiety.

"I did." But Alex was not willing to throw away Mike's chance to win the bake-off because of their meddling. "How closely were you eavesdropping while Grandpa was telling his story?"

"Close enough." Chloe gave her a cautious look. "What do you have in mind?"

Mentally Alex summarized the information she had just become privy to. She realized the one ingredient Mike needed might not have to come from either Chloe or her grandfather.

"There's someone else in the big chocolate picture. Uncle Sal has just become a player."

"You're crazy. Sal is the cause of all this," Chloe said.

"But he can be the solution too."

"Where are you going to find him? Nobody has seen this guy in years."

Alex knew exactly where to start. All she had to do was convince her friend Sarah to find a crack in her professional confidentiality and tell her how they could contact Mike's elusive Uncle Sal.

Chapter Nine

Horoscope: Share a sweet treat with a friend.
Be open to where it might lead.

Even after the distasteful scenario at the chocolate shop, Mike felt like he had a triple-espresso shot of luck. He had decided to stop by the firehouse and pick up his new duty roster when Alex's best friend and confidante had offered to walk with him. But he soon realized that the energetic little chatterbox was not going to willingly offer him any insight to her friend's existence, here on earth or in outer space. She did, however, reinforce what he already knew about Alex's loyalty to Max.

It wasn't in Mike's nature to pry, so he let Sarah chatter away about the neighborhood and its recent renovation. She seemed to know a lot about the businesses on Smith and the surrounding streets, as well as the merchants and their private lives. But she still wasn't talking about the Martinellis. If she had any insight into the feud between Sal and Max she was guarding it well.

A block away from the firehouse, Sarah's cell phone rang. Mike stepped back a polite distance but still heard every word she said.

"Alex." She seemed surprised to be getting a call from her friend. She winked at Mike and signaled she would just be a minute.

Mike suspected this woman never had a short conversation in her life. However he was just a little curious as to why Alex was calling so soon.

"Wow, that sounds like a possibility." Sarah glanced at Mike and smiled.

Were they talking about him? He felt just a little uneasy not being able to hear the conversation on the other end.

"No, I can't. Not now. I've got to pick up the monthly receipts from Bloomberg's Bakery and get them back to the office." Sarah looked pensive. "I realize we've got a time restriction. How about dinner?"

What could have possibly happened in the short amount of time that it took them to walk two blocks. Mike shrugged it off to women and their addiction to the telephone. He was, however, curious as to where they would be this evening.

Sarah didn't disappoint him. "Luigi's at eight. Ciao, see you there." She glanced in his direction. "By the way, Mike says hi."

Mike pictured Alex on the other end of the phone, her cheeks turning cherry red.

"Don't be silly," Sarah whispered. "He didn't hear a word."

This time Mike was sure the question was about him.

Sarah slipped her phone back into her bag. "I've got to run. There's some unexpected research I have to do. It was nice meeting you." Without coming up for air she continued, "Hey, why don't you stop by Luigi's later?"

"I've got dinner plans," Mike lied. The only plans he had were to pick up a pizza, a six pack, and get a good night's sleep. Of course he would have preferred a romantic dinner with Alex, but a threesome was not his thing. And the guys at the firehouse would be expecting him to check Alex's charts before he ventured forward with any type of date.

"Oh, you've got a date." Sarah didn't hide her disappointment.

Mike chuckled and shook his head. "No date." Sarah might be disillusioned if she knew he hadn't had a date in months.

"Then there's no reason why you can't stop by for dessert." She smiled, turned, and walked away before he could answer.

Mike wished the guys at the firehouse would forget their silly bet. He preferred to use his own free will and judgment to win Alex's affection. There was still the old man. He doubted even the heavens could help him convince Max his intentions were honorable.

Inside the firehouse, the engine and ladder teams were

out. By the look of the dried-up pasta and sauce, it looked like they were having a busy day.

Mike decided to pick up his roster and leave. Getting into his locker was going to be difficult. The guys had plastered the door with checkout counter books on sun guides to romance, Chinese horoscopes, and an assortment of daily, weekly, and monthly charts.

"Very funny," Mike said out loud. He pulled the books off one by one. They were so small they fit easily in the palm of his hand.

He placed them in an empty shoebox he found on the bottom of his locker. One of the books flipped open and caught his attention. *If You Love a Scorpio Woman* stared at him in bold black type.

He straddled a bench in the corner and thumbed through the little book. Maybe there was something to this hocus-pocus. The page he read described Alex so well. "If you want a relationship with a Scorpio woman, be patient and persistent. Trust doesn't come easily, especially if she's been burned."

She'd been burned all right. Mike couldn't help but think of her relationship with that pompous plastic surgeon. He read on.

"She might even prefer a life of dateless Saturday nights to another bad situation."

That was exactly how he felt. They had more in common than he imagined. This stuff wasn't so far off. Mike walked back to his locker and opened his recipe book where he had tucked Alex's star chart for safekeeping. What did Nilda have to say about today?

"Scorpio (Nov 7): It isn't really a good day to start a new romantic relationship."

Once again the words rang true. Even though her eyes told him one thing, he knew the scene in the chocolate shop would put a wedge between them. Alex was true to her sign. A close relative of the spider. Drawing him close with a magnetism he couldn't resist. Then quick to retreat once she was threatened.

"Okay Miss Nilda, you're the expert. What do you suggest I do?" He stared at the star chart.

Mike was no longer alone. The teams were back.

"Who ya talking to?" Ralphie walked up behind him.

The smell of smoke and sweat filled the confined space. Mike knew only too well the tired expressions the men around him had on their faces.

"Bad day?" Mike asked.

"Sixth alarm of the day." The engine driver looked exhausted. "This one was a seven story multi-dwelling on Third Avenue." He glanced over at Mike's locker and his expression changed. He smiled. "I see you got our little love note."

"Whatcha gonna do about it?" A member of the ladder team sat down next to Mike. "Our bet started last week." He glanced at the calendar over their heads.

If joking with Mike helped elevate their moods, he'd let them have their fun. "It's the seventh." He pointed to the calendar. "Don't worry guys, I'm way ahead of you. Alex and I have a dinner date."

Ralphie had lifted one of the little books and began

reading. "To avoid being alone, have dinner with a friend and dessert with another."

The captain took the book from Ralphie and said, "Friendship is a start. Remember the guys' bet is not about finding a new friend. But I'll give you this one." He reached in his pocket and tossed a five-dollar bill in the helmet.

Mike smiled as the other guys followed the captain's lead. Everyone here had visited the burn unit to see a buddy or someone they rescued. Whatever doubts he had about the bet were pushed from his mind.

"Don't worry about it. Everything is coming to-gether." Mike tucked the chart back into the most secure place he could think of—his recipe book.

"Hey, Mike which one are you, dinner or dessert?" someone shouted.

"C'mon, guys. You know I'm not the kiss-and-tell type."

Loud whoops and whistles followed Mike out of the firehouse.

With his recipe book securely under his arm, Mike walked the short distance to his car. If traffic was light, he would have more than enough time to drive home, shower, and be at Luigi's to have dessert with Alex.

Alex arrived at Luigi's before the dinner rush. She planned to be early enough to get a table for two out of earshot of the other diners. The last thing she wanted was for someone in the neighborhood to overhear her conversation with Sarah.

Punctual and ready to work, Sarah arrived at exactly 8:00. Her suggestion to move to a bigger table in case they needed room for the papers she had brought made sense to Alex.

Sarah had come through. A registered letter had been sent to Sal at his last address, somewhere in the Caribbean.

"Don't you send his checks someplace specific?" Alex took an extra sip from her wine.

"The checks go direct deposit to Caribbean Bank in the Cayman Islands."

"Does he make withdrawals?"

"That's privileged information between the bank and their customer. I've done all I can." Sarah rearranged her silverware. "I've probably stepped out of bounds as far as exposing my client's trust. But . . ." She dropped her fork on the table. "It's for a good cause, love between two people who belong together."

"Sarah, this is not about romance or love. It's to help Mike win his baking contest. Have you forgotten what he plans to do with the money?"

"Yes, yes, it's a very noble cause. That makes it even sweeter. It's a win-win situation for everyone. He'll love you all the more. The recipe and the prize money are a given." Sarah put her hand over her heart. "And you'll be reuniting him with his long lost uncle."

"You are definitely going overboard this time." Alex

released a long sigh. "I'm not interested in Mike's gratitude."

"I should hope not, there's a lot more to that man to be interested in."

"Oh, Sarah, you're sounding more and more like Chloe."

Sarah tossed her straight brown hair over her shoulder. "How would I look with purple highlights?"

Alex giggled and picked up her menu. "Let's eat."

Sarah, who was usually famished at dinner, ate deliberately slowly. Alex found the leisurely pace welcome after the events of the past few days.

When the waiter cleared the table, Alex reached for her wallet.

"Wait," Sarah said. "I feel like dessert tonight."

"You never eat dessert."

"And you never date fircfighters."

"I'm not dating a firefighter."

"Don't lie to me, Alex Martinelli. You know if that Mike guy asked you out you'd reconsider your ridiculous vow." Sarah looked at the waiter and said, "Bring us a dessert menu."

Over her menu Alex watched her friend. She seemed a bit on edge, glancing at her watch and then over her shoulder at the door.

"What is with you all of a sudden?" Alex asked.

"Let's order dessert." Sarah snapped her fingers to get the waiters attention. "How long will the apple tart take?"

"About ten minutes to prepare." The waiter cleared

their table and explained, "We like to serve it hot so the ice cream can soften as you eat it."

"Perfect. Bring us each a cappuccino while we're waiting." Sarah ordered for the both of them.

"Cappuccino, an apple tart with ice cream—what's going on?"

Within seconds of asking the question, Alex followed Sarah's gaze to the door. Mike Simone held the door open for an attractive redhead. As the redhead slivered by Mike, Alex felt her stomach do a flip. This was a popular place and anyone could come here on a date or whatever. Just because a guy acts like your hero, rescues you a few times, and smiles at you in a way that makes you weak-kneed, it doesn't mean you have any claims on him.

"Hey, look who's here." Sarah stood up and waved at Mike.

He spotted them and walked toward their table. Alex relaxed when the redhead walked off in the opposite direction and joined a man with three equally attractive auburn-haired boys.

The realization that she had just been jealous of the idea of seeing Mike with another woman left her speechless.

"Hi," he greeted her with one of his meltdown smiles and pulled out the chair across from Alex. Suddenly the spacious table seemed smaller.

"So glad you could make it." At least Sarah was open and honest about inviting him. "We were just about to have dessert."

Alex found her voice. "I'll get the waiter, and you can order."

"You can have my share." Sarah stood up and gathered her papers and pocketbook. "My eyes are always bigger than my stomach. You two sit and enjoy yourselves. There are some facts I have to check for Alex."

Alex wasn't sure what to think when Mike didn't try hard to convince Sarah to stay.

Dessert came and Alex realized Mike might prefer a slice of chocolate cake instead. "Maybe you'd like to order something else.

Mike took a sip of the steaming latte and said, "This is fine. I love apple pie and ice cream. I don't mind sharing, unless you want to eat it all."

Alex laughed. "Actually I don't think I can manage more than a taste." She gestured at the sinful presentation in front of them. "Dessert was Sarah's idea. Wait until I get my hands on her."

Mike stared at her. She waited, afraid of what he was thinking. He was too nice of a guy to be put in a predicament that would force him to say or do something he didn't really want to. After the incident in the chocolate shop, he might just prefer to keep away from anyone named Martinelli.

Whatever she had said seemed to amuse him. The corners of his lips tilted in a smile. "Remind me to thank her." He picked up two forks and handed one to Alex. "Dig in," he said.

Alex waited, letting Mike take the first taste. She rested her chin in her hand and watched, mesmerized as his senses appeared to burst with the flavor. Did he sample everything with such gusto?

"Alex, you have got to taste this." He closed his hand over hers and guided her to the dessert plate. "Quick, before the ice cream is too soft and you lose the sensation of the combined textures."

"Oh no, I've already eaten too much."

"C'mon, you have to try this." He handed her a fork.

There was something about the playful way his hand closed around hers as he guided her fork forward. His eyes teased her in a way that made it impossible not to accept his offer.

A shiver of excitement ran through her. His touch lured her to share the experience with him. With his hand still on hers, she brought the fork to her mouth. He leaned across the table. Her pulse quickened. She let him guide the pie and ice cream past her lips. He was so close, she could smell the clean scent of his after-shave. Her lips tingled, and not only from the perfect blend of the melting ice cream against the warm tart.

He released her and smiled. "Perfect, isn't it?"

"Delicious." She swallowed slowly, wanting to hold onto the moment.

Mike watched her, staring at the base of her throat where her pulse beat, as if her heart had left her chest.

"Wow, this is definitely not your average pie à la mode." he dug his fork into the remaining dessert.

When he pushed the plate forward to offer her the last piece, she politely refused. "I don't think I could handle any more of that."

He smiled at her in a way that said he too was enjoying more than the dessert. "There's only a small piece left."

"You have it." Alex reached for her fork and pierced the tart. She was about to bring it up to his mouth when the peaceful chatter of the other diners was overshadowed by a loud screech. At the other tables conversations stopped, forks paused in midair, and everyone turned in the direction of the window and the sound of screeching brakes.

Adrenaline rushed through her veins. Alex sat on the edge of her seat.

Mike was already out of his chair. "I guess dessert's on hold."

Instinct dictated her response. "Hey, wait for me." She pushed aside the unfinished tart and followed.

Outside the restaurant Alex stood back and looked at the scene. The incident was far worse than she could have anticipated. Crushed metal and broken glass were all over the street. A white SUV appeared to have rolled over. Skid marks lined the street from the car behind, which hit the back of the upside-down vehicle, sending it further down the street.

A small crowd had gathered. Mike announced he was a firefighter and people stepped aside to let him pass. He ordered someone to call 911, then asked the witnesses for details. His tone was reassuring, and everyone started talking at once.

Impressed by the obvious confidence he inspired, Alex listened as the driver of the second car, his hands clasped to his head, attempted to explain what had happened. Still dazed by the incident, the man walked back and forth repeating, "I couldn't stop. I just couldn't stop in time."

Mike listened and tried to calm the man. But it was a distraught young woman who caught their attention. "My sister, Betty, she's still inside." Tears rolled down her checks. "I tried to get her out but she's stuck." The woman looked directly at Mike, grabbed his hand and pleaded. "You've got to help her."

He didn't hesitate. The next thing Alex saw was Mike rushing toward the overturned vehicle. She raced after him. "What do you think you're doing?" She couldn't hide the panic in her voice.

Mike looked at her with a crooked smile. "Don't worry about me." He reached out and cupped her chin tenderly in his hand. His eyes were wide with determination and courage. Around them a hushed crowd waited. For a brief moment they looked at each other as if they were alone on the street.

"I might be able to get her out. If I can't, at least I can offer some comfort."

"I smell gasoline." Alex sniffed the cold air. Gasoline was leaking, and he was about to crawl into the vehicle.

"Even more reason why I can't leave her alone in there." In a gesture to silence her protest his fingers slid across her lips in a movement that was almost a caress. "No time to argue."

Alex thought of her rescue and how safe and secure his sudden appearance in the smoky ER made her feel.

Then she reminded herself, just like she did every time Chloe went off on her, that Mike was just doing his job.

A warning voice whispered in her head, *Be smart. Stay with the crowd.* She had no intention of obeying her sensible inner voice. What if there was something she could do? She left the safety of the crowd and rushed toward the overturned vehicle.

She knelt down alongside the crushed passenger door and watched Mike carefully inch his way into the overturned SUV. He had to be careful because a wrong move could upset the balance.

"Is she okay? Is she conscious?" Alex held her breath and waited for an answer.

"Hi, my name's Mike." Mike spoke to the victim. "I don't think I can get you out but I'm going to stay with you until the rescue crew arrives."

From her position Alex could see the flickering lights on the crooked dashboard. Mike had positioned himself flat on his stomach and faced the victim. If the woman was conscious, she would surely respond to that handsome face beside her. Hoping to get a better glimpse, Alex moved to the front of the vehicle.

Mike must have sensed her move and said, "Alex, now that you're here stay to the side."

From somewhere in the crushed vehicle a soft frightened voice said, "Thank you."

Alex turned to the anxious sister and said, "She's alert. That's a good sign."

She accepted a blanket from someone in the crowd. It was a handmade child's quilt. She hesitated before taking it but the stranger insisted. When she bent down to pass it to Mike, she heard him talking about his family. He seemed to be saying anything that came to his mind. Alex was impressed. Whatever worked to get the lady's mind off her dangerous predicament.

"Are you married?" he asked.

"Yes, fifteen years." Betty's voice broke. "Will someone call my husband?"

"Don't worry. I happen to know from a good source that when fire rescue arrives, they'll handle everything." Mike's voice sounded so calm and in command even Alex found herself relaxing.

"Here's a blanket." Alex passed the quilt over the broken window.

"Watch the glass, Alex." Mike's voice was full of concern.

"Is that your wife?"

Alex heard Mike laugh. It didn't seem like such an outlandish question. Why would he think it was so funny?

"Did you ever hear of the Hatfields and Mccoys?" Mike asked.

"Those feuding families?" Betty managed a soft chuckle. "I think Romeo and Juliet sounds so much more romantic."

"You're right. I like Romeo and Juliet much better."

Alex felt a flash of resentment over his comment about the feuding hillbillies. After all, it was his uncle who stole the recipe from her grandfather.

Thinking of her own problems at a time like this was

inappropriate. Arguing about who did what to whom would have to wait. And yet, it seemed strange that this tough firefighter would think of the story about their rival families to use as a distraction. Did he really think of them as Romeo and Juliet?

Flashing red lights reflected off the broken glass. The ambulance and fire truck had arrived. She had to applaud their response time, even though it seemed like forever since Mike crawled under the car.

"Hey, Alex, is that you?" Ralphie helped her to her feet. "That could only mean Simone's inside the vehicle."

"Why would you say that?" she asked, wondering if it was her own uneasiness being with Mike that made her suspicious of Ralphie's assumption.

"I don't know." Ralphie shrugged. "You two seem to be thrown together in these kinds of situations a lot lately."

Behind her, firefighters and paramedics were running and shouting orders. She turned and saw Mike had emerged from the overturned vehicle. He stepped aside to allow the rescue team room to work. Seeing him standing there safe and intact made a strange feeling well up inside her. A strong emotion sent her racing toward him. Standing on tiptoe she threw her arms around his neck and touched her lips to his. At first his mouth was firm and his arms remained at his side. Of course he was surprised by her actions.

He reached for her. With his calloused hands he cupped the back of her neck. His lips softly pressed against hers, demanding more than the simple kiss she offered. She felt her knees weaken as his arms crushed her into the firm contours of his powerful body.

How she wanted to give herself to the passion of his response but she knew she shouldn't. He was a Simone. Brave, handsome, and caring—he still was a Simone. Her thoughts churned. The reality that she couldn't hurt her grandfather was dragged from a place in her mind that was ruled, not by impulsive actions and emotion, but logic and reason.

Ever since she was a little girl, her entire family flinched whenever the name Simone was mentioned. If she did such a stupid thing as fall in love with a Simone, they would never forgive her. She pulled away.

The crowd around them didn't see the inner torment her kiss had stirred. They mistook her action and began applauding. They saw her kiss as nothing more than a reward for his heroic actions. But would Mike? After the way his lips moved over hers, she was still trying to convince herself that her impulsive action was no more than a response to his bravery. Who was she kidding?

The paramedics had Betty on a backboard with her C-spine immobilized and an air splint on her left leg. Before being lifted into the ambulance, she demanded a moment with Mike. He gracefully accepted her thanks before the doors closed.

Sirens blared and lights reflected off the shop windows along the street. A fire truck prepared to turn the vehicle upright. The crowd remained. But Alex had seen enough.

"Hey, I owe you dessert." Mike stepped behind her and kneaded her shoulders.

His touch reminded her of the intimacy of his returned kiss. She wanted to turn and run before she was in too deep.

"No thanks; I should be getting home." She turned to leave and bumped into Luigi, the restaurant owner.

Luigi threw his hands in the air. "How wonderful. You are both so brave." Looking over his shoulder he expected them to follow inside. "Come, come. The chef will make you a special dessert. Would you like a flaming soufflé?"

Mike gestured with a sweeping motion of his arm for Alex to lead the way.

She looked at him and paused. Heat surged through her and it wasn't from the image of the flaming soufflé, "I can't play with any more fire tonight."

"I know it sounds cliché but . . ." Mike's eyebrows arched mischievously. "I play with fire all the time."

"Sorry, not tonight." Alex hugged her arms close to her body. While logic was still in control, she turned and walked away.

She just knew Mike had to be a fire sign. She would bet he was an Aries, an all-or-nothing kind of guy who wouldn't settle for just being friends.

Alex knew in the cosmic dating plan, an Aries and a Scorpio were a difficult love match. Difficult, but not impossible.

Chapter Ten

Horoscope reading: Misunderstandings
can be set straight now.

Mike's shift was over and most of the other guys were catching a few winks. It had been two days since the night of the accident, and he hadn't spoken to Alex. Unfortunately, several of the guys were out with the flu, so Mike agreed to pick up a few extra shifts. The days had been filled with too many calls and long hours. Mike hoped he had enough energy to drive home.

Exhausted, the guys still managed to keep a close watch on how their bet was going. Every day he found daily horoscopes cut out of the local newspapers. Today little grocery store books were tossed all over the kitchen table. Just for the heck of it Mike picked one up and decided to check his sign—Aries. Skimming over the rubbish about his finances or his health he found what really mattered—romance.

He read some malarkey about the sun being in position to rule his love life, giving him a creative attitude toward romance. Yeah, he'd give them that one. If he stretched it, using Alex's horoscope might be considered creative. Blah, blah, blah, he read on. Now here was something that he liked.

He read out loud, "You're determined to find your soul mate and build a lasting relationship." He skimmed down the page, disregarding the nonsense about Venus and Mars. At the bottom he read again. "Despite her independent nature, Miss Right makes a devoted, understanding mate." Right on target in describing Alex's personality.

He flipped the page. *If she's a Capricorn, flirtation could lead to a potential relationship.*

With Aquarius expect friendship. No way. The last thing he wanted was to be Alex's friend. His body responded to the vivid recollection of kissing her the other night. Her kiss had been good and sweet. But when his lips responded he sensed her urgency as she melted against him. He groaned and threw the little horoscope book across the table.

It didn't say anything about a Scorpio in his future. So what. He was much too sensible to believe in any of this stuff. But if the guys weren't going to let it go, he was still obligated to continue with this hocus-pocus courting.

He pulled out Nilda's chart and set his plan of action

for this evening. *Take the strain off your relationship. Speak your mind to set things straight.* If he stretched the prediction, he could make it apply to their going-nowhere relationship.

He knew Alex was as attracted to him as he was to her. Her resistance had nothing to do with the alignment of the stars. She let that silly feud between her grandfather and his Uncle Sal put a wedge between them.

It was time someone got to the bottom of this and Mike decided he was the only one who could do that. But how would he find his Uncle Sal after all these years? No one in his family had seen or heard from him. And they liked it that way.

Alex sat in the waiting room of the rehab center waiting for her grandfather to finish his whirlpool treatment. He had the last appointment of the day, so the therapist took a little extra time with him. She picked up a copy of the *Post* and skimmed through the pages. After reading her horoscope, she hoped to find some news about the lady pinned in the overturned vehicle the other evening.

In the local section she found a tiny article. The piece stated how after forty-eight hours of observation, the woman was discharged home with a few scrapes and abrasions and a broken leg. She did make a statement thanking an off-duty firefighter and his girlfriend who helped her remain calm while waiting for fire rescue to arrive.

Alex smiled at the reference to Mike as her boyfriend.

It wasn't such an unpleasant thought, but one she couldn't consider. If anyone reading the article knew anything about her loyalty to her family, they would realize how unlikely such a union was.

She did however wonder why she hadn't seen or heard from Mike. The bake-off was less than a week away, and she was sure he would return to the Chocolate Boutique to at least talk to Chloe.

Alex glanced at her watch. Office waiting rooms were terrible places with nothing to help pass the time but outdated magazines. She picked up last month's *Financial News* and stared at the cover. She thought of Sarah. She hadn't heard from her since they agreed to contact Sal.

Alex reached for her cell phone and dialed her friend. She could use a little good news at the moment.

"Hi, Alex. I can't believe it's you. I was just about to call you." Something big must have happened because Sarah was ranting on and on. "You'll never guess who's in town."

"Who?" Alex played along.

"Sal, he's here. He's in New York. Right here in Brooklyn."

"No way." Alex never imagined their plan would succeed. "What should we do next? I can't just walk up to Sal and say, 'hi, I'm Max's granddaughter. You remember him. You stole his chocolate recipe and we need it back. Oh and by the way I'm falling in love with your . . .'"

A door opened, distracting Alex for a moment. Had she just confessed her feelings for Mike out loud? She looked up and saw her grandfather and his therapist approaching.

"Hellooo . . . Are you still there?" Sarah's voice echoed.

"Sarah, I can't talk now. Meet me at the chocolate shop later. Bring Sal. I've got to go." She flipped her phone shut.

"How'd the session go?" Alex tried to sound calm, meanwhile her insides were churning.

"*Phh.* How do you think it went?" Grandpa waved his clean bandage at the therapist. "This young man says I've got to keep coming here for another two weeks. What's he think, I've got nothing better to do?"

Alex gave the therapist an apologetic glance.

"Don't worry about it, I've got a grandfather too." The therapist patted Max on the back. "But my grandfather can't make chocolate like this man can. I asked him . . ."—he leaned closer and whispered—"what's the secret? But he won't reveal the ingredients. I never realized chocolate-making was shrouded in such secrecy."

"Oh, you couldn't imagine how exclusive some of the recipes are." Alex tried to force a smile and make light of the therapist's remark. "Grandpa is one of the best at keeping those old recipes locked away."

"And who would you have me share my years of work with?" Grandpa retorted. "That handsome fireman you get all googly over?"

"Time to go. Thanks for your help." Alex ushered her grandfather out the door. Was it so obvious how Mike affected her that even her grandfather noticed?

Outside the medical building, Max turned in the direction of his store.

"Grandpa, the bus stop is the other way." Alex wanted to go home and change before meeting Uncle Sal. She even considered contacting Mike. They might need him if things got sticky.

"Have you forgotten it's Thursday, our late night?" Max asked. "We still have time to stop at my candy store. I can hang around until closing."

Alex was afraid he might ask questions if she suggested going home first. She offered no argument and followed her grandfather. A cup of Chloe's hot chocolate might be just the thing to brighten her woe-is-me mood.

Along the streets the air was filled with the smells from a variety of ethnic restaurants. As they walked the short distance from the rehab center to the store, Max chatted on and on about the old neighborhood. Alex had heard the details many times and nodded politely as he pointed to a trendy boutique that had once been a ma-and-pa grocery store.

"Now here's a building that hasn't changed." Max pointed to the firehouse.

Alex looked up and saw Mike coming out of the side door. He carried a duffel bag in one hand and tossed a ring of keys in the other. She glanced at her watch. His shift had just ended. Her grandfather was a little ornery at the moment and maybe it would be better to avoid a face-to-face meeting at this time.

Mike turned to speak to someone, and she lost sight of his somber but still handsome face. She still, however, had a view of his broad shoulders tensing as he lifted the duffel bag and tossed it to the man behind him. Who was she lying to? It wasn't her grandfather's remarks she was afraid of. Somehow Mike managed to remain polite and respectful no matter what her grandfather's accusations. What disturbed her was the unnatural way her heart thudded when she saw him.

With her hand on Max's elbow, she guided him to the opposite corner. She tapped her foot impatiently while she waited for the traffic light to turn green.

A gentle but firm tap on her shoulder made her turn. Mike had noticed them. Even after what must have been a hectic day she saw a restless energy in the way he shifted his weight.

"Hi." Mike looked down at Max's fresh bandage. "How's the hand, Mr. Martinelli?"

"How do you think it is?" The light turned and Max stepped off the curb. He turned to Alex and asked, "You coming?"

"I'll be right behind you, Grandpa."

"Have it your way." Within seconds Max disappeared into the rush hour crowd, leaving Mike and Alex on the corner.

"I get the impression Max can be difficult. You've got the patience of a saint." Mike's gaze was riveted to her face, then moved down her body slowly. "You look good in spite of everything that's happened to you."

"So do you. I mean you look a little tired but . . ." A cool wind blew between them and some curls escaped from under her hood.

Mike reached up and brushed the loose hair back into place. His hand rested on her cheek. "Alex, we need to talk about what happened the other night."

"The lady you helped get through that horrible ordeal is doing fine. I read it in the paper," she said, trying to ignore how his touch made her pulse pound and yearn for more.

"I'm not talking about some stranger. I'm talking about us. Something happened that night, and you can't deny it."

"Oh, that kiss? It was nothing." In a casual gesture she waved her hands through the air. "I'm sure you've been thanked in many ways by people you've rescued. I acted impulsively. It was nothing more than a reward for your bravery." She couldn't tear her gaze from his face and wondered what he would do if she stood on her toes and put her lips on his. She knew exactly what he would do. She was foolish to even be thinking such thoughts.

"Why don't I believe that?" He raised a brow in amusement. "If your impulses are packed with that much emotion I want to be around when you put some thought into it."

She wanted him to be around too, but circumstances had dictated otherwise. There was no denying they had both liked that kiss.

The traffic light changed to green. Around them, unseeing New Yorkers waited to cross the busy street. As the crowd closed in around them, they were forced to cross or be trampled. Mike reached out and caught her hand in his. The simple gesture and the touch of his hand was almost unbearable in its tenderness.

On the other side of the avenue they stopped in front of a fancy paper boutique. Her back to the store window, Mike rested his hand on a metal grating and leaned close. His free hand slipped up her arm bringing her toward him.

Her body tingled from the contact. How was she ever going to convince, not only him, but herself as well, that they were wrong for each other? "This is not just about us. There are so many other people involved."

"Who?" The determined look on his face told her he wasn't falling for any more of her lame excuses.

"There's Josh."

"Oh really. Your ex-husband?" Mike's smile returned. "You're going to have to come up with a better excuse than him. I think you're avoiding the real culprits."

"You mean Max and Sal?"

"Yes, my uncle and your grandfather. Two old men who have a half-century old quarrel that seems to be keeping me from moving on with my plans." Mike ran his hand over the top of his buzzed hair.

"Your plans?" Alex paused. "Oh, for the bake-off."

"And other things." He looked her dead in the eyes. A pulse beat in his neck. He wanted to kiss her. She could tell by the way he stood close but not close enough to reach her lips.

Mike was right. An ancient feud had them stuck between the past and their future. She, however, was glad the conversation had taken a turn. "Why don't you ask your uncle?"

"It's easier said than done. My elusive uncle has never been very popular with my family."

"Is it because of what he did to Max?"

Mike laughed. "I didn't even know my uncle knew your grandfather. I knew he grew up in the neighborhood, but I didn't know he was connected to your grandfather until that day at the fair. My family has bigger issues with him."

It had never crossed her mind that Mike might not want to see his uncle. She let out a sigh, suddenly feeling deflated. There was no time to contact Sarah. She was probably on her way to the chocolate shop. What had seemed like an excellent idea the other day now had the potential for another disaster. When had the stars turned against her?

"What did Sal do?"

"It's more like what he didn't do." His dark eyebrows slanted in a frown.

Oh no, she thought, *this isn't going to be good.*

"Are you okay?" Mike asked.

"I'm fine." She forced a smile. "Please, I'm anxious to hear about this family issue."

"It's no big deal. You know how big Italian families can be. You miss a funeral, and they hold a grudge forever."

"That's it? Your uncle missed someone's funeral?"

"Well." Mike cocked his head to the side. "It wasn't just anyone's funeral." He glanced at his watch. "You got time for this story?"

Alex adjusted the collar of her jacket to ward off the shiver that ran down her spine. "This is as good a time as any."

"You look a little cold. Maybe we should talk about this over a cup of coffee." His fingers brushed her neck as he helped her adjust her hood.

"No, I'm fine," She lied. Her heart thumped erratically from his touch.

"You can sit and watch but I could use a cup of coffee."

She didn't need warm coffee. His touch kindled feelings of fire, warming her from head to toe. Unfortunately she didn't have the luxury of lingering over a steaming latte while she listened to Mike confide in her about his family skeletons. There was too much at stake. At this very moment, Sarah could be walking into the Chocolate Boutique with Sal.

"Oh no." She didn't mean to speak her thoughts out loud but her grandfather was on his way to the store, alone. She looked at Mike. His closeness gave her mixed feelings of security, and yet, uncertainty. She wanted to stay but knew too much depended on what she did next. As she always did, she did the right thing and stepped away from the protection of the storefront.

"Change your mind about the coffee?"

"Your story will have to wait. I've got to catch up with my grandfather before . . ." She looked over her shoulder and the flicker of disappointment in his blue eyes ripped through her like the chilly autumn wind. She hoped she wouldn't regret what she was about to say. "Meet me at the chocolate shop around closing time."

There would be two possible scenarios by the time Mike showed up. All the old wounds would somehow be miraculously resolved, or more likely, he would walk into a whole new bag of gummy worms.

No doubt the universe wasn't working in her favor. She realized she hadn't been thinking clearly ever since she met Mike Simone.

Chapter Eleven

Horoscope reading: Your first quarter moon is "crisis in action." Don't be afraid to accept your fate.

Lost in his thoughts, Mike created the illusion of isolation on the crowded avenue and followed his usual path to Mulligans Bar. Mulligans, a hangout for off-duty firefighters and police officers, was the perfect place to kill some time before meeting Alex.

As he approached Third Avenue, he noticed a group of construction workers heading into Mulligans. An idea came to him. His sister, Kate, was working a site near Pacific Street. He'd give her a call and ask her to meet him for a drink. He hadn't seen her in a while, but that wasn't his only reason for making the call. Kate, the family historian, might have a different slant on the Uncle Sal issue. When she was in college, she spent one spring break on Sal's boat sailing around the Caribbean. Mike remembered how he had anticipated his turn to visit their beachcomber uncle. It never came.

The next year their grandfather, Sal's twin brother, passed away. Sal sent his condolences weeks after the family buried him. No one believed Sal's story that he hadn't received the message, no one except Kate. Her fond memories of the week she had spent with Sal were never discussed again.

"How's the job going?" Mike ushered his sister toward two empty stools at the end of the bar. He wasn't here to drink with the guys or have them ogle Kate.

"Good." Kate gave him a curious look. "Since when are you interested in the business?"

Mike smiled. This was his older sister he was talking to. She would see through any lies. "Actually I need some information on Uncle Sal."

"Sal?"

"Yeah, Sal." Mike had to be at the candy shop in an hour and didn't have time to waste. Getting right to the point he asked, "Did you know that Max Martinelli and Sal had some kind of falling out? Max won't even speak Sal's name?"

"Martinelli, that old candy kook?" Kate shrugged. "All I know is that everyone likes the Simones, whether it's business or pleasure. Everyone except Max." She gave him a curious look. "Why you asking?"

"The few short encounters I've had with the old man, and I mean short, have been anything but pleasant."

"Why would you ever cross the old man's path. I don't remember you being fond of all that fancy candy. If I remember correctly, Snickers were always your favorite."

"My tastes have changed." Mike clasped his long-neck beer and regrouped his thoughts. "I kinda met him through his granddaughter."

He thought of his first glimpse of Alex at the fair and their recent conversations. His patience was an asset, up to a point. Unlike some of the guys at the firehouse, he wasn't the kind to give up just because he hadn't won her over right away. A meaningless fling wasn't what he wanted with Alex. Proving something to his buddies wasn't even a thought. It was all about making himself happy. The problem was how to convince Alex she had to do the same. He took a sip of his beer and smiled. Maybe using her star charts wasn't such a bad idea. He planned to give her all the time she needed to realize they belonged together.

"Is that silly grin on your face what I think it is?" Kate snapped him out of his private thoughts. "Your sudden interest in the old man wouldn't have something to do with the granddaughter?"

He put the beer bottle on the bar and nodded. "I'd like to soften the old man's attitude toward me. Maybe you can shed some light on the feud."

Kate laughed, making no effort to suppress her amusement. "I can't believe my still-single brother is attracted to the only woman in the whole city who's related to Max Martinelli." Still giggling she asked, "How did that happen?"

"I was on detail with Danny at the fair when I saw her. I knew I'd find a way to speak to her." He shifted on the barstool. "This may sound ridiculous but it was almost like fate or something when I responded to the fire at the candy booth. You know all that stuff about the proper alignment of the planets and stars. Everything seemed to fall into place after that incident." He continued telling her about the ER fire.

"Fate?" Kate laughed so hard her wine sprayed Mike. "Since when do you believe in all that hocus-pocus?"

"Don't go there, Kate. The moon will have to rise over asparagus before I believe all that stuff."

"You're reading the daily horoscopes?"

"I only read Alex's horoscope so I can make good on the guys' bet."

"What bet?"

Mike reached into his back pocket and pulled the star chart out of his recipe book. "All I have to do is follow this chart for one month."

"You are crazy. What if she finds out?"

"There's no reason for her to ever know about the bet."

"Aren't you ever tempted to see what the stars have to say for you?" Kate raised a brow and smirked.

Mike suppressed a smile. "Occasionally." He wouldn't admit to anyone but Kate that he had read his horoscope. And the bet—the whole thing with the bet still tugged at his insides. If the guys hadn't sweetened the deal with their generous donations, he would be tempted to call it off.

"Who would ever believe my gorgeous little brother is going to all this trouble for some girl? She must be really special."

"She is." Mike wasn't here to talk about Alex. He hoped his sister could shed some light on the family's feud with Sal. Something from a woman's point of view that might soften Alex's perception of the man her grandfather despised.

"What can you tell me about our elusive Uncle Sal?"

Kate didn't know any family secrets that Mike hadn't heard before. She did, however, have a suspicion that Sal and their grandfather, Sal's twin brother, had some kind of falling out years ago, before Sal took off. So Max Martinelli was not the only one who had a falling out with Sal. If only Max would talk and shed light on the entire Uncle Sal puzzle.

Kate sipped her wine and studied Mike over the rim. She shifted on her stool and said, "I'm impressed by what you're doing. All this for some girl."

Mike knew that look. She had a knack of knowing which of his girlfriends were serious and which ones were only out for a good time way before he did. "You'll like her. Next time we meet I'll bring her along."

"Who are you trying to convince?" She gave him a knowing smile. "How are you going to get her away from the old man?"

"Don't worry. She'll come around." Mike wasn't sure

he should be so confident. Alex had been increasing on edge the more he spoke about Sal.

"And that would be when?" Kate laughed then added, "When the planets align with asparagus."

Mike shrugged. "Whatever it takes."

"You are serious, aren't you?"

He glanced at his watch. "I'm going to meet her in about an hour."

"You'd better get going. Women hate men who make them wait." She signaled for the bartender to bring their tab. "This one's on me."

"Thanks." Mike made his way toward the door.

Outside the sun had set and the evening chill hit the back of his neck. He took a moment to adjust his collar. He was about to cross the street when he heard Kate calling his name.

She approached at a steady jog. Something must have happened. She looked at him with a flicker of amusement. "You are not going to believe this. Mom just called."

"Is everything okay?"

"Fine, fine." She waved her hand casually in the air. "The last person you would ever suspect to see just showed up at her door."

Mike had no patience for riddles. "Who are you talking about?"

"Uncle Sal's at Mom's house."

"What's he doing in Brooklyn?"

"That's the best part. He's here to see you. For some strange reason he thinks you need his help."

"Me? Why would I need help from someone I haven't seen since I was a kid?" Kate had the reputation as the family practical joker. "Are you baiting me? Setting me up or something?"

"You called me, asked me what I knew about our Uncle Sal, and he shows up minutes later. Who's baiting who?" She raised a suspicious brow. "This wouldn't have anything to do with that girl, the horoscope chick?"

"I'm as surprised as you are." He ran his hand under his collar and asked, "Any idea why me?"

Kate shrugged. "I would suggest you cancel your plans for the evening and find out what this is all about."

Mike reached into his pocket and pulled out his cell phone. He started to dial the number for the chocolate shop and hesitated. Kate's suspicion could be right and Alex might be behind their uncle's sudden appearance. He put the phone back in his pocket.

But how and why? Could his elusive uncle possibly be here to help him with his chocolate recipe? Wow, that wouldn't sit well with Max.

Kate hailed a cab. Mike climbed in behind her.

"Any hint of strange visitors in your horoscope today?" Kate giggled.

"Get over it," he said. But actually the words in his horoscope just took on new meaning. "You have a hard time accepting help. You'll need to take a leap of faith to achieve the give and take of a lasting relationship."

"Leap of faith," Mike said out loud but Kate didn't notice. She was busy giving the driver instructions which streets to avoid during rush hour.

Maybe all his past girlfriends were not solely to blame. He had never been so committed to making things work as he was with Alex. For some cosmic reason, he knew seeing his uncle was the first step. The call to Alex could wait until tomorrow. The only thing marring that decision was the knowledge that she would be waiting for him at the candy shop. There was also the chance the meeting with his uncle could somehow be damaging to his relationship with Alex.

Alex would have to wait.

"Alex, you have to stop pacing." Chloe gripped her shoulders to keep her in place. "They'll be here soon." She nodded in Max's direction. "Want him to get suspicious?"

"Who do you think will show up first, Mike or his Uncle Sal?" Alex looked out the window at the half moon. The astrological definition of first quarter moon was "crisis in action." She turned away, afraid to think of the possibilities. One potential disaster did cross her mind and she asked, "What if they show up at the same time? Mike, Sal, Max."

Chloe threw his hands in the air. "This is turning into an M&M nightmare." She shuddered. "Peering out the window won't bring them here any faster. I know, watched chocolate never melts."

Sweet Chloe, trying to keep it together for her sake. If she showed the least bit of anxiety, Max would immediately sense something was up.

Alex looked out the window again. Rush hour was

winding down. A late straggler wandered into the chocolate shop. He was a man of about forty. Too young to be Uncle Sal. Alex wished he was. She felt her stomach knot every time the doorbell announced another customer.

Chloe poured the man a cup of her steaming chocolate. She signaled for Alex to follow her to the counter where she offered her a cup of her comforting brew.

As Alex approached the counter, the sweet smell of rich chocolate had an opposite effect on her. Her stomach churned. She refused the mug Chloe offered. Afraid she might have hurt her feelings she looked up to explain. "My stomach is a little queasy."

"This whole thing is making you sick, isn't it?" Chloe's thin brow knit tight, and she looked at Alex with concern. Ever since the incident in the ER she had looked at Alex the same way whenever she thought Alex might be having some ill effect from the smoke. "I never saw you refuse a cup of my hot chocolate."

"It's not what you're thinking. I'm just a little edgy about this meeting. Mike didn't seem too thrilled when I mentioned his uncle. He hinted at some old family squabble or something." Alex tried to force a smile. "I just want things to work out for everyone. If Sal gives Mike the recipe then Grandpa can't find fault with Mike. Maybe he will even forgive Sal."

"But if Mike is not too fond of his uncle . . ."—Chloe shook her head—"things could be very bad.

The phone rang. Alex and Chloe jumped.

Max gave them a curious look and picked up the

receiver. "We're closing soon but if you really need those receipts for tomorrow, I'll wait around." He hung up the phone and said, "That was Sarah. She's on her way here. Said she's missing some of last month's receipts. You two can go. I'll close up."

"Oh, no. We'll stay," Alex said.

Max shrugged and walked over to the table where their last customer had finished his hot chocolate.

Alex watched her grandfather carry the dirty cups into the backroom. His gait was slow and tired. It had been a long day. The doctor's appointment to check his wound, followed by a whirlpool treatment, had taken its toll on him. Was she doing the right thing?

It had been a long day for everyone. She pulled out a chair and sat down.

Chloe carried two steaming mugs to the table and shoved one under her nose. "I know what you're thinking," she said. "Having Sarah bring Sal here is beginning to feel like a very bad idea."

"If Sal had made his choice to come here from his own free will, the whole situation might not be such a mess. But I interfered." Alex twisted a paper napkin into a tight ball. "Inviting Mike is interference on my part too." She put the napkin on the table. "He didn't refuse. He was more than willing to meet me here." It was not like Alex to second guess herself, but she had never been in such a sticky mess before.

"He thinks he's coming here because you want him to." Chloe watched her over the rim of her mug.

Chloe's scrutiny made her uneasy. She shifted in her

chair and tried to think of something to help her out of this mess. "There are other outside powers that could have dictated this meeting."

"Oh, yeah. I don't think Max was about to send for his arch-nemesis." Chloe leaned across the table and said, "This is real life, babe. Not some scene out of an astrological comic book."

Alex looked at Chloe, surprised by her sudden take-charge attitude. She couldn't agree more. "Reality stinks doesn't it?" Alex said.

Alex was about to take a sip from the hot cocoa Chloe had forced into her hands when the door opened again. She glanced at the chocolate Kiss clock. Two minutes until closing. This had to be them. She clutched the oversized mug, allowing the warm surface to give her a moments reprieve before she turned.

Sarah walked through the door. Alex held her breath and waited to see who followed. No one came in behind her friend. She was alone. Perhaps they had devised a plan, some kind of signal that would tell Sal it was okay to enter. Yes, that had to be Sarah's plan or else they would already be inside the chocolate shop.

Chloe must have read Alex's mind. She pushed Sarah aside and stuck her head out the door. "Where's Sal?"

Sarah closed the door behind her and said, "I'm sorry. He's not coming. He had some important family matters to settle first."

"What do you mean, Sal isn't coming?" Alex put her hand to her throat and whispered, "I told Mike to meet me here at closing time."

"Hurry up and call him." Chloe handed Sarah her cell phone. "Tell him not to come. Max is still here."

"Calm down," Sarah said. "Mike's not going to show up either."

"He's not?" Alex felt relief mixed with disappointment.

"No." Sarah glanced worriedly at her friend. "I'm sorry. Sal wanted Mike to act as a mediator with the family. Once I explained the whole chocolate scenario Sal saw the opportunity to make amends with his family by helping Mike."

"Maybe my grandfather is right about the man. Sounds like Sal has pissed off a lot of people." Alex gave Sarah a wary look. "Your chocolate connection again? Only this time it's about to melt in a messy puddle."

"How can you say that? Sal is here, in Brooklyn. He's meeting with Mike. So what if he shares the chocolate secret with him a little earlier than you planned. Isn't that what you wanted? To get this whole sticky mess out of the way so you and that handsome firefighter can move on?"

"The other day it seemed like a good idea." Alex pressed her fingers to her forehead and pictured Mike leaning over her: tall, smoky, and gorgeous. "If he gets the recipe he won't have any reason to hang around here anymore."

Sarah gave her friend a cross look. "You really believe the recipe was the only reason he's been stopping by here?"

"No. Mike's the most amazing guy I ever met." The

ring of the cash register made Alex turn away. Her grandfather removed the evening sales slips from the drawer. She turned back to Sarah and said, "Even so, a nice guy like Mike is only going to listen to so much of Max's bad mouthing his family before he gives up."

"Mike's not a quitter," Sarah whispered as Max approached. "And neither are you, my friend. Don't give up on this one; he's worth the effort. If I were you I'd call that man and tell him the truth about Sal's unexpected visit."

"You're crazy." Alex laughed. "And he'll think I'm crazy too." But how would Mike react if she came right out and confessed that she had taken it upon herself to bring his estranged uncle back to New York? While she was making a fool of herself, why not admit she had fallen madly in love with him.

Chapter Twelve

Horoscope: Keeping secrets is a wonderful trait.
But when you're in love, not letting your romantic
interest in on the news could be a problem.

Alex sat at the nurses' station staring at the computer screen. Picking up an extra shift proved to be an inadequate distraction from Mike Simone and the whole chocolate recipe mess. Aside from her disappointment in not seeing Mike last night, she almost hoped his Uncle Sal had given him the recipe and was on his way back to the Caribbean at this very moment. Then no one would know she had plotted with her friend to bring Sal here. So many things could go wrong. What if Sal was too old to remember the recipe? He could harbor hostile feelings toward his family and not care about Mike winning the bake-off. Even more disturbing, what if his anger toward Grandpa Max had festered over the years?

It was too late to agonize over all the sticky scenarios. Sal was here and needed to come face to face with her grandfather. Mike needed to get the chocolate recipe, and most important, this sticky mess needed to be resolved so she and Mike could go forward with whatever destiny had planned.

She remembered too well the sensation of responding to the firm contours of Mike's body. It would be easy to say it was all physical attraction and not meant to be anything more. But Mike was more then a handsome face. He was kind and caring. He liked kids, he put up with her cranky grandfather, and never minded how tired she looked. Never in her wildest dreams did she think Mike would have this impact on her thoughts. Well, maybe in her wildest dreams.

"Are you charting or day dreaming?" The unit secretary tapped her on the shoulder. "You've got a call. Someone with a very sexy voice." She smiled and added, "Could it be that good-looking firefighter?"

"You guys are as bad as Chloe." Alex reached for the phone, curious and just a bit apprehensive as to who was on the other end. "Hello, this is Alex. How can I help you?"

"Hey, Alex. It's Mike."

She felt her mouth go dry. Maybe she should just confess that bringing his uncle here was all her idea. Too late to be sorry. She had acted impulsively and intruded in his personal life. If he never wanted to see her again she would understand.

"Alex, are you still there?"

"I'm here."

"You're probably busy so I won't keep you long." His voice sounded deep and sensuous. "I'm sorry about last night."

"No big deal. I didn't wait long." She answered in a suffocated whisper.

He continued, "Can you meet me at Max's store after work? There's someone I'd like you to meet."

Alex wasn't sure of her exact words but she knew she had agreed to meet Mike.

At about 3:00, the flow of patients in the ER slowed down. The nurse manager, in hopes of containing her budget, offered the nurses a chance to take some time off. Alex jumped at the chance. She had slept poorly the night before and didn't want Mike to see her looking so tired. The few extra hours would give her time for a quick nap, a shower, and the opportunity to meet Uncle Sal dressed in something other then her baggy scrubs. Yeah right, like she really cared what Uncle Sal thought.

Mike seemed to always see her under the most unusual circumstances. He had seen her at her worst, overcome with smoke then flat on her back vomiting into a bucket, even upside down peering into an overturned vehicle. For such a sensible man he sure had a warped sense of what he found attractive.

At home Alex found a note on the kitchen table. Her brother had taken Grandpa Max to his PT appointment. He planned to drop him off at the store afterward. How could she have been so stupid to ignore the possibility that her grandfather would show up at the chocolate shop?

So much for her plan to look appealing to Mike. A few bad comments from her grandfather and Mike might not care if she was a Victoria's Secret model. Even if Sal had smoothed things over with his family and given the recipe to Mike, a meeting with her grandfather was still necessary. Despite her good intentions, she still felt edgy about telling Mike she had interfered.

Things didn't look any better after she had rested and showered. She couldn't do this alone. Chloe, of course, would be there but she'd be of little help if things got nasty. She picked up the phone and dialed Sarah's cell number.

"Pick up the phone," she pleaded into the receiver. After the fourth ring she realized she would be on her own tonight.

Alex walked the distance to the store. She needed time to regroup her thoughts and think of what she would say. *Keep it simple,* she thought. *Let everyone else carry the ball. Just respond appropriately. Yes, that was a good plan.* She increased her pace. Of course she knew all her well-thought-out plans would melt away the minute she entered the shop and actually faced Mike and his uncle.

Outside the shop, Alex hesitated. Chloe stood behind

the counter waiting on a young couple. She breathed a sigh of relief that her grandfather was nowhere in sight. Alex felt the blood drain to her feet when she spotted Mike and an elderly gentleman seated at the corner table. Mike always managed to look so calm while she felt like a huge cosmic explosion was about to unravel her from the inside out.

The older man next to Mike looked nothing like Alex expected. Sure, he was tan and wrinkled from the sun, but his tailored wool coat and felt hat were stylish. Nothing like the bohemian look she imagined. His blue eyes, however, sparkled like diamonds on the ocean. Grandpa had been right, there was no mistaking the man's resemblance to his nephew.

Mike noticed her and rushed to the door. Alex tensed when he reached for her elbow, pulled her inside, and guided her toward the table.

"You're not going to believe it. My Uncle Sal is in town." When she didn't reply, he added, "You know the guy your grandfather is always calling a thief."

Alex took in the playful look in his eyes. Obviously he didn't take her grandfather's accusations as serious as she did. He didn't seem the least bit bothered by his uncle's appearance after all these years. Maybe things went well last night.

Mike almost dragged her to the table.

The elderly man in front of her looked kind. Nothing like the monster her grandfather had portrayed him to be. Would this pleasant-looking man be able to sugar-coat her grandfather's feelings. Who was she kidding?

Any minute Grandpa Max could walk through the door and the whole scene would be charged with his anger toward his old friend.

Mike, calm as ever, continued with an introduction. "Alex, this is my Uncle Sal."

Sal eased himself out of his chair and extended a weathered hand.

She was about to reach for the outstretched hand when the bell over the door announced a new customer.

Alex knew before she looked, it wasn't someone in need of a chocolate fix. Grandpa Max had just come in. She turned and saw the look on his face. Tension charged the corner of the shop.

It seemed like an eternity but actually took only seconds for Max to cross the floor.

"What are they doing here?" In two long strides, his overcoat flapping behind him, he was at Alex's side. With a light tap he pushed Mike back and pulled Alex away before she could shake Sal's hand.

"I don't know what any of you are up to but I've got my suspicions." Max glared at Alex. Over his shoulder he snapped at Chloe, who maneuvered herself toward the back of the store. "Don't even try to leave."

"Isn't it time you put this silly feud behind you?" Alex, embarrassed by her grandfather's response, wanted desperately for everything to work out.

"Never. I'll take this to my grave." He pointed his bandaged hand at Sal. "You had better leave. Whatever these kids told you, you were a fool to believe."

C'mon, Max. It's been too long since we've seen

each other." Sal bowed his head in greeting. "These young people have good intentions. Don't you think we should help them out?"

"What'd they tell you?" Max barked.

"Can't an old man decide to visit his friends and family and try to make amends for his past?"

"*Phh.* You expect me to believe you've developed a conscience."

"Okay, so maybe I had a little coaxing. It seems my nephew needs some help with a chocolate recipe." This time Sal pointed an accusing finger. "Maybe if you weren't so ornery and unwilling to let go of the past you'd help him out."

"You want them to think it's only about the recipe, don't you?" Max glared at Sal.

Biting her lip, Alex asked, "Is there more?"

Her grandfather turned away. He looked at Sal with a fiery, angry look she had never seen before. "You're still the same charmer with the ladies. They're always taking your side. Didn't you learn when it cost you your relationship with Gladys?"

"Gladys? My grandmother?" Alex grabbed Mike's arm.

"We've all done things in the past that we're sorry for." A tormented look crossed Sal's brow. "I wish she was still around so I could ask her forgiveness." He shuffled his feet staring down at his shoes. "Who'd she end up marrying?"

Grandpa's voice cracked, "Me."

Sal hesitated. "She wouldn't have been happy leaving

her friends and family," he said defensively. When he looked up his expression had softened. "She definitely got the better man."

It was Mike's turn to react. "Wow. There's more to this feud than some old recipe. You guys were involved in some romantic triangle over Alex's grandmother?" He placed a protective hand on Alex's shoulder and asked, "Did you know?"

Mike's comforting touch reassured her that somehow she would survive this evening. "I had no idea." She would never have asked Sarah to contact Sal if she'd known her grandfather's resentment ran deeper than the silly recipe feud.

"Ah." Grandpa Max looked at her and Mike. "You kids think you invented love and romance." He gave Sal a cautious glance.

Silly, inconvenient tears stung Alex's eyes. She felt guilty and selfish. Her grandfather was not as oblivious to his surroundings as she believed.

A quick glance at Mike took her by surprise. For a moment she was caught by the look in his eyes, an emotion so strong it pulled at her heart. Before it swallowed her whole she knew she had to do something.

Chloe was already on it. She cautiously approached the group with some mugs and a pot of her famous hot chocolate. The steam from the enchanting blend mystically rose above the cups.

"Why don't we all sit down and have a soothing cup of Chloe's hot chocolate." God knows we can all use some of the magic, Alex wanted to add, but kept her thoughts to herself.

"Take the chocolate away." Grandpa Max stood at the edge of the table refusing to budge. "All my secrets are out in the open." He pointed an accusing finger at Sal. "You should have stayed away."

"Stop being such a cranky old man. A lot of chocolate has melted between us since I left." Uncle Sal offered Max his hand. "Give the kid our recipe and . . ."

Max's face was bright red. "I think you've got things backward. It was never our recipe. It was mine. I shared it with you." Through stormy eyes he looked up at Mike. "I can't believe this old thief hasn't given you the recipe yet."

"Well, sir, he . . ."

"He doesn't remember it." Max wouldn't let anyone finish what they had to say. "Should have known. Steal it, sell it, and forget it. Just your style."

"Grandpa, shouldn't you at least listen to what Sal has to say?" Alex had never seen this side of her grandfather.

Sal stepped around the table, face to face with Max. "Smart girl, must take after her grandmother." He did not seem like the type to stand there and take a beating, verbal or otherwise.

Max did not back off. He stood toe to toe, face to face with Uncle Sal and shouted, "Well, go ahead! What do you have to say?"

"Will I'm sorry be enough?" Sal stepped back.

Max also stepped back. His shoulders sagged. All the years of secrets and anger had left a toll on his tired, old body.

Alex stepped forward, but Mike's strong grasp held her in place. "Don't interfere," he whispered.

If Mike only knew how she had orchestrated this entire meeting he might not be so supportive. She shook her head and watched her grandfather prepare to leave. Torn between the obstacles that had gotten her in this mess in the first place, she attempted to pull away but Mike slipped his arm around her waist, locking her in place.

Grandpa Max surprised her. He did not rush forward and attempt to push Mike away. He buttoned his coat and turned toward the front of the store. At the door he stopped and looked back over his shoulder at Chloe. "Give the kid the recipe."

"Grandpa, you really mean it? Mike can have the recipe?" Alex released a long slow sigh. Her plan was a success. Or was it? She and Mike could move on but what about Sal and her grandfather?

"Maybe your uncle should go after him." Oh God, there she was interfering again, but someone needed to do something. She turned to Sal. "You still have things you need to explain. Don't you?"

"Lots of years to catch up on." Sal nodded. "Max and I have old wounds to heal but you youngsters have the future to discuss." He put on his coat, and in a stiff shuffle, Sal rushed after his friendly enemy.

There might be some more arguing, but Alex had a

feeling things would work out between those two old cronies. They appeared to have been made from the same mold.

Mike helped Alex carry the mugs, still full of hot chocolate into the back where Chloe was cleaning up. A chilly autumn wind blew through the open back alley door.

Mike walked over and closed the door. "It's getting cold out there. Can't imagine that my needing a chocolate recipe would be reason enough for my Uncle Sal to leave those balmy breezes this time of the year." He knit his brows in a pensive expression. "How'd he even know I needed help?"

Chloe coughed and almost lost her hold on her precious chocolate pot.

Alex gave her a cautious look.

Chloe got the hint and changed the subject. "The contest's only a few days away. Now that I have Max's blessing, I'll give you all the help you need." She shut off the lights and went to open the cash register drawer.

It took several minutes for Alex's eyes to adjust to the dark. Mike's fingers closed around her arm as he guided her around a table. Moving slowly, she allowed him to lead her to the front of the store.

Streetlights lit the front window. Mike stood close. Too close.

To break the edgy silence, Alex said the first dumb thing that came to her mind. "I'm glad my grandfather agreed to give you his recipe. Where do we go from here?" Too late she realized how her last comment must have come across. She looked at him and noticed a sly smile on his lips.

"I was hoping we'd go back to my place," he whispered in her ear.

She forced herself not to respond to the softness of his breath across her face. Tired and overwhelmed from the emotionally charged evening, her back ached between her shoulders. "I'm talking about the bake-off."

"We could still talk about the bake-off." His hand brushed across her back, lingering too long.

Alex exhaled and relaxed into his gentle massage. One little yes and it could be the perfect end to an almost perfect night. He might not even care about her part in his Uncle Sal's sudden appearance. Her body yearned to accept his invitation. Her heart beat fast from the possibilities. She waited until her spinning senses came to a halt before she responded.

She exhaled, turning the conversation back to his cake. "Is there anything in the rules that states you can't use the recipe?"

"I guess that's a no for tonight?" One hand still lingered on her back. With his free hand he reached into his back pocket and pulled out his recipe book. "I might have a copy of the rules with me." He gave her a sideways glance. "Sure that's what you want to do right now, read some boring rules?"

"What I really want to do is go home and get into bed."

"Bed sounds good to me too." His lips curved in a seductive smile. He loosened his grip on the book. A few sheets of paper slipped onto the floor.

"Are those all the rules?" Alex attempted to catch the pages as they fluttered to the floor. "Seems like an awful lot to remember."

"No." Mike was faster. He had the papers in his hand before she could reach them. "This is something else. I've got a copy of the rules back at the firehouse."

"Something important?" she asked, trying to get a glimpse of the loose pages.

"This?" He held the papers over her head out of view. "It's nothing. Just a firehouse joke." His tone quick and conclusive signaled that he didn't want to discuss whatever was on these pages.

But something looked familiar and piqued Alex's interest. In the dim light it was difficult to see, but she thought the format resembled a horoscope chart. What was Mr. Asparagus doing with one of Nilda's star charts? She still didn't know his sign and this might be the perfect opportunity to find out. Curiosity wouldn't allow her to let this go. On her toes she reached for the papers.

"Is that your horoscope?"

"An asparagus star chart? Don't be ridiculous." His attempt to sound nonchalant sounded forced. He tucked the paper into his back pocket and reached for his jacket.

"Then whose chart is it?"

"What makes you think it has anything to do with that hocus-pocus you take so seriously?"

"I know a horoscope chart when I see one." She watched him slip into his leather bomber jacket. Let him have his secrets, after all, she still hadn't admitted her part in bringing his uncle here. She busied herself with the buttons on her coat while Mike hung the closed sign on the door.

"How are you getting home?" Mike asked.

"I'll walk or catch a cab."

"Why don't you walk back to the firehouse with me? I parked my car outside."

"What about Chloe?"

"Don't worry about me." Chloe suddenly appeared. "I'll catch a cab on Atlantic."

"I'll share a taxi with you," Alex offered.

"No, you can't." Chloe's response was quick and abrupt.

Alex, not sure if Chloe had overheard Mike's suggestive invitation threw her an are-you-crazy look.

"I'm going in the opposite direction. You know how cab drivers are late at night." Chloe smiled at Mike. "You should take his offer."

Alex, too tired to argue, nodded in agreement.

Mike insisted they walk Chloe around the corner. They waited while she hailed a taxi.

Once Chloe was safely tucked into her cab, Alex and Mike turned the corner in the direction of the firehouse. A cold wind pressed against them, pushing Alex back. Mike offered her his hand. She reached out and curled her fingers around his strong, calloused, yet comforting fingers. He closed his grasp, and Alex sensed he wasn't going to let go, even when the wind died down on the main avenue.

"If my uncle is smart he'll head straight back to his

warm paradise. I still can't understand what possessed him to come north this time of year." He stopped at the corner and looked at her. "Maybe we should go with him."

There was no escaping Mike's curiosity about his uncle's decision to visit New York. Alex freed herself from his grasp. "Mike," she said, not sure where she was going to begin.

The light turned green. He stepped off the curb. She reached out and put her fingers around his arm. Beneath the soft leather of his jacket his powerful muscles kneaded to her touch.

He stepped up on the curb, closer until their bodies almost touched. She took a breath; a cold sting of air filled her lungs. There was no going back. She had to say what she planned to say and get it over with.

"I'm the one who brought your uncle here." She prepared for the worst. "Do you think I was meddling?"

He glanced at her hand clasped tight over the sleeve of his jacket, took his other hand from his pocket, and snaked it around her waist, pulling her close.

"I think your meddling was fine." He looked sincere.

"I did the right thing?" she asked. "I know your family has issues too."

"You did the right thing." He lowered his head and kissed her.

The whole Uncle Sal incident seemed so trivial as he caressed her lips with a series of slow, shivery kisses. There were no excuses now, no interfering relatives or old feuds to keep them apart. She didn't even know his sign. Was she compatible with an asparagus? Their lips seemed to be.

A driver of a black SUV honked at them. Alex pulled away but didn't get far. Mike held her hand.

"You're sure you're not upset about Sal showing up?" she asked one more time for reassurance. If he wasn't bothered, there was no need for her to agonize over it.

"Why would I be? Everything turned out fine. With Chloe's guidance my cake will win first prize and . . ." He pressed a kiss in her palm before adding, "I've already won my prize."

"I couldn't handle a relationship that wasn't open and honest." Her hands slipped around his hips. The crinkled edges of his recipe book scratched her fingers. "No secrets?"

Mike tensed. He released her. "Absolutely, no secrets."

"Good. Why don't you tell me what someone born under the sign of asparagus is doing with a star chart."

"Trust me." He kissed her forehead. "Forget about it. You really don't want to know. It's just firehouse humor." The yellow light blinked. He rushed her across the street.

She wanted to trust him. If they got seriously involved, it sounded like that was his intention, and if he did something that went against everything she found good about him she would kick herself for ignoring the signs. She didn't want him to be just another almost relationship that went bad.

She had to trust him, forget the silly paper, and let

him have this little secret. At the firehouse she waited outside while he went in to gather his gear.

The contest rules were still on the table next to untouched plates of dry macaroni and cheese. The guys were out on a call. In the center of the table sat the worn helmet overflowing with cash.

Alex's questions had gotten too close to the subject of the bet. He almost confessed, but couldn't let the guys down. They contributed generously every time he was with Alex. The pot had grown substantially.

If love did make the world go round, his love life would just have to hang in a precarious orbit a little longer. Just until the bake-off was over and all the prizes were his.

Chapter Thirteen

Horoscope: Let your senses experience
the world around you. Don't mistake a new found
harmony for happiness.

Sensory overload assaulted Alex as she entered the huge armory hall where the firefighters were already deep into the bake-off. Rich smells: vanilla, cinnamon, and, of course, chocolate filled the room. Cheery hostesses in fire hats and bunker pants tempted the visitors with trays full of high calorie, but irresistible samples.

Alex passed a server carrying large chocolate-glazed puffs. Thick cream oozed from the sides. Much too big. Another tray passed. Cups of gooey chocolate tempted her. Much too rich. She continued to look around the area, searching for Chloe's signature decoration on a brick-shaped piece of chocolate cake. There didn't appear to be any left. Could be a good sign.

Might as well sample the competition. Feeling like a traitor, she plucked a zebra brownie from a passing tray.

The striped top layer satisfied the taste for both chocolate and cheese. "Delicious." She pushed a stray crumb into her mouth.

"They're all perfect." A hostess overheard her comment. "I'm glad I'm not a judge."

Alex hated to agree, but the server was right. Competition would be stiff. She hoped Chloe and Max had been able to help Mike enough to give him a competitive edge. She refused any more tempting treats. Too many samples were not only bad for her waistline, but increased her apprehension that Mike might not take first place.

She left the tasting area. The neatness of the competitors' work areas conveyed a sense of control in the vast room filled with an array of spectators. From her past experience at chocolate competitions she assumed this crowd was a mix of cooking students, friends and family, and dessert foodies.

Several rows back in the audience she spotted Mike's support system, the guys from the firehouse and his Uncle Sal. Danny saw her first and waved. He held a big sign over his head: Bring Home the Bake-in Mike.

After sampling the competition, Alex didn't have the guys' sense of confidence. There was a good chance Mike would not bring home the prize.

A voice blared over the loud speaker. "Ten more minutes."

Alex squinted at the clock in the back of the room, then down at the competitors. Would Mike finish in time? Apprehensive, she approached the section with Mike's friends.

"Why do you look so worried?" Uncle Sal moved over a seat allowing Alex to sit between him and Danny. "Chloe's watching our boy like a mother hen. They've got everything under control."

"Have you tasted the samples?" She glanced at her watch. "I never expected the competition to be so steep."

"Don't let the time remaining worry you. Watch that boy at work." Uncle Sal pointed to Mike. "He's like a fine sculptor."

A large overhead screen projected an image of each of the contestants at work. Each contestant was required to prepare three entries: one for the judges, one for the photographer, and a third for eating. A close-up of Mike working on his last cake covered the screen. The crowd cheered. He was obviously the audience's favorite. Would the judges agree?

Alex looked up at the large screen, then down to the baking floor. She watched Mike bend over the table. Gosh, he was made to wear fitted jeans. With a quick twist, he turned the brim of his firehouse cap around so he could get closer to the cake. On the large screen she watched his steady hand square off the corners of the layers. He had nice hands too.

Behind her two female voices let out a loud yell, "Go Mike!"

A tinge of jealousy hit Alex and she turned for a view of Mike's cheering squad.

"Hi. You must be Alex," the older of the two women introduced herself. "I'm Mike's sister, Kate. This is my daughter, Nicole."

Alex exhaled, trying to prevent the color from rising in her cheeks. "How do you think he's doing?" She glanced at the clock again and shifted in her seat.

"He's way ahead of the bakers on each side of him," Kate said.

If Alex hadn't had eyes just for Mike and been so busy checking out his body she might have noticed the beefy firefighter to Mike's left hadn't taken his cake from the oven. But when he did it wasn't applause or cheers that flowed from the audience. Gasps of horror roared from the stunned group. Flames soared through the oven door. There was a shocked look on the poor man's face as he slammed the door shut to contain the fire. Like the other horrified contestants stationed near the flaming cake, Chloe stood protectively between the stations.

Fool, what did she think she could do if the fire got out of control? Mike, however, did not seem the least bit bothered by the events. He continued to nip and tuck at the layers of his cake as if nothing happened around him.

Alex sat on the edge of her seat while Danny and the chief raced to the baking floor with fire extinguishers. Even with the flames contained, a pending doom was still possible. The heat could trigger the sprinkler system, ruining the entire contest. A crew positioned on the floor already had the situation under control. The burnt cake, covered in foam, was disqualified but the bake-off would continue.

"That was close." In a reassuring gesture, Kate put her hand on Alex's shoulder. "A stray ash or a little smoke and Mike's cake could be out of the running. The ten thousand dollar grand prize would have gone up in smoke."

"I've been there before." The minute Alex saw the flames she experienced a feeling of deja vu. "The day Mike and I met, my grandfather lost his truffles because of a careless fire."

Kate smiled knowingly. "So I heard."

And what else had Mike told her? Kate had seemed like she was greeting an old friend when she introduced herself. "Your brother seems to have a knack for show-ing up at all the right times."

"He said it has something to do with the universe and the proper aligning of the stars that put him in the right place at the right time." Kate laughed. "I can't imagine my rational brother believing in fate. You must have a strong impact on him."

"I just want to help him win the prize money."

Kate raised a brow. "Really? I think Mike is inter-ested in more than just winning first place."

"He told me how his first partner was treated at the burn unit." Alex understood where Kate was trying to take this conversation, but she wasn't sure herself where her relationship with Mike would go. "If he wins, the prize money is a generous donation. His intentions are noble."

"Very noble." Kate was about to say more but Danny and the chief returned to their seats.

"The contest continues," Danny said. "You ladies talking about the prize money?"

"And other things," Kate said.

"It's not only the bake-off money Mike will have when he wins. We've got a pot back at the firehouse. He'll have a hefty donation for the burn unit at County."

"Are some of the guys betting against him?" Alex knew the guys at the firehouse could be back breakers. "Did someone set odds on which medal Mike would win?"

"Sort of." Danny elbowed the chief. "The guys know there's more to this wager than just baking a winning cake."

The fire chief gave Danny a cautious look.

Alex waited for Danny to elaborate. He sat down without saying another word.

What was that all about? What else would the guys feel was worthy of wagering their hard earned money on? Alex didn't have a chance to ask. The completion bell sounded. Anxious contestants moved their displays to the judging table. They stood behind their entries and waited to be introduced.

Mike stepped back with his hands clasped behind his back. Alex couldn't imagine standing there while judges tasted and commented on something she had worked so hard to create.

The close-up shot of Mike's cake projected on the large screen got a round of *oohs* and *aahs* from the chocolate lovers in the audience. Alex beamed like a proud parent.

"Looks good enough to eat," Danny said.

"I hope the judges think so." Alex watched Mike cut thick slices. He handed one to each judge.

The judges took only small bites. One judge lifted his fork to his nose and sniffed each entry before tasting. No problem there; Mike's cake appealed to every sense.

"Did you see the look on Carla Creek's face? You know, the pastry chef from the cooking channel?" Danny nudged Alex. "She really likes our boy's cake."

Like Macy's mannequins, the contestants stood behind their entries. The audience waited in silence as the judges continued down the line. Alex didn't have any interest in the other contestants. Her eyes remained on Mike. She had noticed Carla too. But she thought her smile was directed more toward the baker than his cake. As the chefs tasted each entry there was no doubting the way Carla keep glancing back that she found Mike as delicious as his entry.

What was it Sarah had said? "Give Mike a panel of female judges and he'll blow the other contestants away."

Alex wanted him to win but not because he was so handsome. Mike wouldn't want to win that way either. Watching him standing there completely undaunted by the other entries she knew he believed his cake was the best.

The audience was asked to remain seated while the

judges came to their decision. A camera crew from a local news station did brief interviews with the judges.

"You seemed to enjoy that beautifully presented seven-layer cake baked by Firefighter Simone." Of course the first question went to the chef who's response to Mike's cake was so obvious.

"The presentation was perfect," Carla answered.

"She should have seen how lopsided his cake was before you helped him out." Danny patted Alex's knee.

Alex had no claim on Mike, but the way Carla kept glancing in his direction annoyed her. She was grateful when the judge, a *New York Times* food critic seated to the right of Carla, reached for the microphone.

"I have no problem with . . ."—he glanced at his notes—"Mr. Simone's perfect rectangular shape but I do believe I would prefer a soft fudge frosting instead of a hard frosting."

"Oh, no, he's going to lose points for the frosting." Alex grabbed Danny's hand. "The frosting was always the issue." She breathed a sigh of relief when Carla took back the mike.

"I disagree. There's an overindulgent thick chocolate butter cream between each of the seven layers. The hard frosting is the perfect contrast. It's almost like eating expensive chocolate candy." Carla glanced at Mike and smiled.

Mike's fans responded with the usual cheering. Alex too applauded, forgetting the seductive looks Carla had given Mike. After all, wasn't that why they were here, so Mike could win the bake-off?

The winners were about to be announced. Alex couldn't remember ever feeling so nervous. She doubted anyone other than Chloe understood all the planning, and as much as she hated to admit it, conniving that had gone in to getting Mike here today.

The announcer stepped forward and wasted no time announcing the winners. "The third place prize goes to Adam Chotiner from Ladder Company number 273, in Queens, for his cinnamon buns."

The remaining contestants beamed smiles of confidence, they were still in the running.

"Second place goes to Lieutenant Chris Jones of Engine Company 33 in Manhattan. His winning entry is from a family recipe for a New York favorite, black and white cookies."

Too many delicious cakes, pies, and cookies were still in the running for the first place prize. Alex's mouth watered as she watched the judges taste those delicious zebra brownies. She watched Mike. He didn't look at all like he could lose, but confident and secure that the grand prize was his.

Alex didn't need any drum rolls. Her stomach churned like a kettle drum as she waited for the first place winner to be announced.

"The grand prize trophy goes to Mike Simone and Engine Company number 204 in Brooklyn. The judges have agreed his seven-layer cake is the perfect combination of textures and taste."

Mike's cheering section couldn't contain themselves. They stood in unison and raced forward to congratulate him. Alex, caught up in the momentum, rushed toward him.

She stood back and watched as he accepted the congratulatory pats on the back and handshakes. When Alex reached him, there were no handshakes for her, he swept her up in his arms and twirled her off the ground.

He smelled as enticing as he looked—like fresh baked cake and decadent chocolate. When her feet touched the ground again, Mike locked a possessive arm around her waist.

"I couldn't have done this without you." He took her hand and led her to the table where Chloe was cutting hefty slices from one of the two remaining cakes. "I want you to have the first taste."

She held the delicate cake close to her mouth and nose, allowing the cocoa blend to assault her senses. Her mouth watered. Alex might not know how to make the chocolate but she considered herself an expert on its taste. A light-as-a-feather cake sat beneath the frosting.

"Perfect," she said through a mouth full of cake.

"Not as perfect as you." His calloused hand took her face and held it gently. He kissed the tip of her nose.

A cameraman noticed them and projected their image over the large screen. After all, Mike had just won the grand prize.

The audience cheered.

Mike glanced up. "Hey, it's like being at a ballgame. Should we give them something to cheer about?" He didn't wait for an answer.

The touch of his lips on hers sent her heart racing.

She didn't care if the entire city witnessed. This was her grand prize. A true Scorpio, she had been suspicious of his trust. Now that everything had fallen into place she no longer questioned his motives. She had worked hard too, dealing with Chloe's hysteria, her obstinate grandfather, and finding elusive Uncle Sal. And most important, never knowing for sure how Mike felt about her. This was her frosting on the cake. Mike did care, and she wanted to let him know she did too.

She stood on her tiptoes, threw her arms around him, and returned his kiss with all the passion she could summon. Her mind faded into a dreamy intimacy until the sound of someone clearing their throat brought her back to earth.

Mike released her reluctantly, and she turned to find Chloe and the *New York Times* critic standing close.

"Sorry to interrupt." Chloe smirked. "The *Times* wants to do an article on Mike for the food section."

"Wow, an article in the *Times*!" Mike seemed almost as excited as he had when they kissed. "I'll need my recipe book."

"Where is it?" Alex asked, afraid if she stayed close to Mike she might do something to compromise her reputation.

"In the back with my extra utensils. There's a box with my name on it."

"Don't worry, I'll find it." Alex took a deep breath, her heart still pounding in her chest.

Behind the scenes did not seem as neat and organized

as the competition floor. To her surprise, her grandfather stood guard over Mike's equipment.

"Grandpa, what are you doing here?"

"That boy needed someone behind the scenes in case of an emergency. Almost had one when that cake burned in the oven." Max shook his head. "Entire contest would have been toast. What're you doing back here?"

"Mike needs his recipe book. Who's minding the store?" Alex knew it was a big deal for her grandfather to leave his shop.

"Nilda offered." He shrugged. "What's the worst that can happen?" He chuckled and answered his question. "She'll eat her weight in hazelnut truffles."

Alex was happy to hear her grandfather joke about his store. She planted a kiss on his cheek.

His smile broadened and he asked, "What's Mike need the book for?"

"Some critic wants to interview him. I guess he needs his notes."

"Look over there in that box. I'm going up front to join the celebration and get in a plug for my shop."

"I'll join you in a minute." Alex spotted the tattered recipe book sitting precariously on top of a pile of cake pans.

Alex reached for the book. The pans slipped off, hitting the floor with a loud clang. She cringed and grabbed the edge of the book. A folded page came loose. Turning the paper over in her hand, she hoped she hadn't disturbed the order of the pages. The paper didn't look like it belonged in a recipe book. The words on the page had nothing to do with baking. It was the chart Mike had dropped the other night. She had been right; it was a star chart.

Hoping for a clue as to what his sign was she scanned the page. The chart didn't have anything to do with Mike. It was her star chart. Puzzled, she read the yellow highlighted areas.

What a Scorpio woman wants from her man is unwavering love and quiet heroism. Be yourself and be her friend.

Confused she glanced over her shoulder in Mike's direction. Tall and proud he was a true hero, surrounded by his friends and family. Not bad for an asparagus.

At first glance it seemed kind of sweet that he would go to all this trouble to get a copy of her horoscope. But why would he highlight some predictions?

Turning her attention back to the chart she read on. On November 7 her horoscope read: *Share a sweet treat with a friend. Be open for where it can lead.*

They had shared a dessert the night of the rollover accident outside Luigis. Was the date November seventh? If they were at Luigis, on the seventh, look where that sweet treat had led.

She doubted Mike would believe the stars influenced the events of the evening. He might have decided on his own to follow her chart, but the accident and their kiss were out of their control. She doubted he would believe it was dictated by destiny.

Although, after the way Mike kissed her, she didn't

need any reassurance. But she was curious to see if her horoscope had guided their relationship. Impressed with Mike's orderly notes, she turned the paper over, looking for more proof that destiny demanded they be together. An odd set of numbers on the back caught her attention. The top of the column read "firehouse pot."

Danny's pot? Could it be the money the guys were betting for and against Mike? Something was odd. The words written next to the dollar amounts never mentioned Mike. Money earned was listed next to each of her daily horoscopes.

Next to November 7, the night she might have kissed Mike, he had written two hundred dollars. Next to other insignificant days there were smaller amounts written in the tally.

Her hand shook. These weren't odds on Mike winning or losing the bake-off. They were betting on her. Rage consumed her as she imagined all the possibilities. Did they wager he would kiss her or was the bet that she would kiss him?

Angry at herself for leaving her feelings so open and unprotected, she tucked the chart between the pages of the book and slammed it shut.

If she confronted him, she was sure he would offer a good explanation. This was not the time or the place. She'd just hand him the book and leave. Would he believe her if she made the excuse that she had to work an afternoon shift? Would he even care? He had won the bet and obviously the money that went with it. And, if the guys had any doubt, she had assured his win by kissing him in full view on a giant screen.

As unlikely as it was that Mike would leave his entourage, Alex turned and found him standing behind her, framed in the doorway, watching her. How dare his strong sexual allure and confidence gnaw at her psyche. Too enraged to see beyond her anger she hardly noticed his blue eyes. The sparkle of winning had vanished.

Mike had almost told her the other night. Now she knew. Her expression ripped at his heart. Not resentful, not sad, or even humiliated. Staring at him, a true Scorpio who had her trust violated, she was just downright angry.

There was nothing he could say, not at this moment. He watched her cross the room in long, determined strides.

"Here's your recipe." She slapped the book against his chest as she walked by.

His muscles tensed protectively. That girl could pack a wallop. He reached for her, only his fingertips brushed her arm. The touch tore at his heart. He wanted desperately to pull her into his arms and kiss away her anger, but she stormed past him, capable of destroying anything in her way.

If Mike had learned anything, he learned that fate was not always on your side.

Chapter Fourteen

Horoscope: Be true to yourself. You are
loyal, determined, and intuitive.

It had been a week since Alex walked away from Mike, but the emptiness that gnawed at her made it feel like months. Once again, she had done the one thing she knew how to do best, throw herself into work.

Alex sat across from Sarah in the hospital cafeteria. Hard as she tried to ignore her friend's persistent comments, it was difficult at the small table.

"You and Mike are acting like overgrown kids. How much longer are you going to ignore each other?" Sarah asked, then added, "The bet was just a thoughtless guy thing."

Alex hated to admit Sarah was right, but she had a hard time dealing with the guy thing. Mike had left her a message the first night, trying to explain how some of the older guys often made him the center of their firehouse jokes. It didn't bother him.

Well, it bothered her. Angry at first, her anger turned to hurt, especially when Mike seemed to shrug it off so easily. At least he could call again.

"Why hasn't he called me? He knows where to find me. If I'm not at work, I'm at the chocolate shop helping Grandpa and Chloe." Alex pierced her lettuce with a little too much vigor, snapping the prongs of her plastic fork. With the broken fork poised over her plate she said, "Do you think he's too busy now that he's an almost celebrity?"

"Could be." Sarah handed her an extra fork. "I read the article written after the bake-off. It's the perfect human interest story at just the right time of the year."

"The article has had a phenomenal impact on business at the chocolate shop." Alex took a bit of her salad. "Sales have tripled from the past holiday season."

"You've got Mike to thank for that." Sarah studied her over the rim of her coffee cup.

Alex couldn't deny her friend was right. Within a couple of days of the bake-off, Mike's interview was in the food section of the *New York Times*. He had done a delicious job blending all the highlights of the feud and the chance rescue of old Max Martinelli at the fair.

"Sarah, you're trying to make a connection between jelly apples and orange slices." Alex pointed her fork across the table. "Whatever you or anyone thought was going on between me and Mike . . ."—she avoided

Sarah's are-you-kidding look and continued—"you're all wrong."

"Sure, whatever you say." Sarah took a bite of her tuna salad. "You know, this isn't bad for hospital food."

There was no way Sarah believed a word of what Alex said. How could she? Alex wasn't convinced herself. But maybe Mike was. Or else he wouldn't have given up so easily. Unless it was true that he was a no good, conniving Simone and used her to win a contest that meant more to him than what she thought they had going on between them.

"So I guess even friendship is out of the question?" Sarah munched on a carrot stick.

"What would Mike and I do as friends?" Alex rolled her eyes. "Share recipes?"

"You're right, friendship isn't possible. How could anyone be just friends with someone who looks like Mike?"

"It has nothing to do with his looks."

"I'll give you that one. There is so much more to the man." Sarah stopped munching and pointed her carrot at the open newspaper on the table. "Did you read this follow-up to last week's article in the food section?"

"No. I've been avoiding the papers." Alex hadn't looked at a newspaper since she found the star chart. Daily horoscopes had lost their appeal.

"It's all about Mike. You're right about his almost-celebrity status. It seems he's attracted a following. Did you know that he had to go on the night shift to avoid the public?"

It was a weak excuse but might explain why he didn't try to call again. Alex knew from firsthand experience how a sudden change to your sleep pattern upset your life.

Sarah read on. "Wow. I guess he's some kind of crazy hero too. Says here how last spring he volunteered to be the first one into a ditch at a collapsed construction site."

"Did he tell the interviewer the story?" There was a lot about Mike that Alex didn't know, but she did know he wasn't the type to toot his own horn.

"No. They interviewed some of the other guys at his firehouse."

Alex reached for the article. The last paragraph concluded with Mike's dream to open a chocolate pastry shop. That was definitely news to her.

"See how little I know about him? I had no idea he wanted to open a pastry shop." She showed the second page to Sarah, circling the last paragraph with her finger. "I can see him being successful at this kind of business."

"So can I. And you, my friend are going to let a man who can bake exquisite chocolate cakes just slip away because of some guy thing?"

"The perfect man does not make you the object of a bet with his buddies."

"I think you're looking at this all wrong. I see it as the financial opportunity he took it for. You helped him earn money for a very worthy cause."

"So like an accountant to bring money into everything." Alex couldn't disagree. The guys at the firehouse had increased Mike's donation to the burn unit significantly.

"I guess I could call, tell him I read the article, and thank him for mentioning Max and Chloe again."

"Do you feel just a little left out since there wasn't even a hint of you in either article?" Sarah asked.

She wouldn't admit, even to her best friend, that she did feel somewhat neglected. After all, she'd played a crucial role in getting Max and Sal together again. Harboring her true feelings she said, "Why would he? I didn't have a secret recipe to share with him."

"Ouch," Sarah said. "You said that with the true sting of a hurt Scorpio."

"I'm not hurt," she lied and stacked Sarah's empty plate on top of her own. "I've got to get back to work. See you later."

Alex returned to the ER just in time to hear the call over the medcom.

"We've got a mass casuality. Can you accept three of the victims from a fire at a renovated building site on President Street?"

With most of the people in the neighborhood out doing last minute holiday shopping, the ER had been quiet and could easily handle three victims.

"What's their condition?" Dr. Frank asked.

"Two stable firefighters and one construction worker found unconscious. Two victims are immobilized with backboards and cervical collars. Vital signs are stable on all three." Before signing off, the dispatcher added, "It was like a Collyers mansion out there."

"What does that mean?" Dr. Frank asked.

The group gathered around the medcom shrugged. Alex was the only one that knew the answer.

"It's fire rescue talk. Collyers mansion describes a place filled to the ceiling with junk."

"And you know this because . . . ?" Dr. Frank gave her a questioning look. "You're dating the firefighter who saved you from the ER fire?"

"No. I'm not dating a firefighter." The group around the medcom looked at her and she blushed. "I know this because when my brothers and I were kids, my dad, who's retired from the department, would refer to our messy rooms as the Collyer brothers' house."

Dr. Frank still looked puzzled so she continued, "I think it happened in the 1940s. You know those pack rats that can't throw anything away? Well, there were these two brothers living in a Harlem brownstone that had papers and boxes stacked from floor to ceiling. Firefighters can't even get in those apartments, not to mention how all that trash feeds the fire."

"I get the picture." Dr. Frank shook his head. "Lets get set up. These guys could be stable now but sounds like they could crash."

While Alex set up her IV drips she realized Mike's house could respond to a fire on President Street. Grateful that she had read in the *Times* article how Mike had been forced to work an off shift, she breathed a sigh of relief. It was only noon. Seeing him as a patient was not how she imagined seeing him again.

The first patient, a construction worker, arrived and

was taken to the trauma room where the team waited. Alex waited in her assigned room for the next patient to arrive. She almost didn't recognize Danny. Covered in soot and smoke, he was immobilized on a backboard.

"Hi, doll." He rolled his eyes and looked at her. "Listen, I'm fine. All this hullabaloo just because I fell through the floor. Can you get someone to get me off this thing?"

"You fell through the floor?" Alex couldn't contain her surprise that Danny was alert and talking. She placed a comforting hand on his shoulder, did a quick assessment of his neurological status, and said, "As soon as we get some X-rays that show nothing is broken, the doctor will clear you. How far did you fall?"

"I feel through the floor but didn't go any place. That crazy boyfriend of yours saved me."

"Mike worked today?" She tried to contain the anxiety in her voice by casually adding, "I heard he was on the night shift."

"He switched with one of the guys on the day shift." Lifting his restrained finger only inches off the backboard Danny tried to point behind her. "I think it's his shoulder. Might be out of joint. He hung onto me for a while, until the guys could reach us."

Alex glanced at Danny's vital signs. Assured that he was stable she turned in the direction Danny had tried to point. An hour ago it might have bothered her that he referred to Mike as her boyfriend. Now, after her conversation with Sarah, she more than liked the idea.

She saw Mike sitting on a hallway stretcher with his

right arm restrained in a shoulder immobilizer. Before she had a chance to approach him, a transporter wheeled him off to X-ray.

Disappointed, she turned back to Danny. He too was on his way to radiology. Before he left the room she heard him say to the transporter. "Imagine being the crazy guy who saved me. Going to all the trouble of being a hero just so his girl, who didn't answer his calls, would notice him." Danny's boisterous laugh followed him down the hallway.

Danny's comment, Alex knew was for her benefit. These guys, no matter what their predicament, always watched out for each other. She walked into the hallway where the walking wounded—firefighters needing treatment for smoke inhalation and minor injuries—filled the stretchers along the wall. She helped move portable oxygen tanks and draw blood.

"Hey, Alex." One of the guys from Mike's house recognized her. "Did you see that boyfriend of yours? He's the hero of the day."

"So I heard. He just went for an X-ray." She placed a saturation monitor probe on the firefighter's finger.

"Did he get a chance to tell you how he saved Danny's life?"

Alex managed a smile. "No, Danny told me."

"How's the old guy doing?"

"Danny's fine. Acting like his old self." She recalled his comment about Mike. "He went to X-ray too."

"Don't look so worried. I'm sure Mike is fine. He's

pulled that shoulder out before. I know him, he probably popped it back in by himself."

She needed to see for herself that he was not burned or suffering from smoke inhalation. A clash of fire and water churned her insides. Mike was so active and passionate about what he believed in. Risking his life, he had all the characteristics of a true fire sign.

Feeling like a jerk, behaving like a true water sign, acting emotional and sensitive, she needed to tell him she was sorry for the way she acted at the bake-off. She understood the bet had been nothing more than friendly banter between the guys. She had no right to accuse Mike of anything else.

She was busy in Room Six, helping the ER doc roll Danny off his backboard so they could inspect his back for any injuries, when she heard Mike's voice. Her emotions mixed with relief made her hand slip along the side of the backboard.

"Be careful; I'd hate to see this big lug fall after all the trouble I went through to save him." He walked toward her and stopped on the opposite side of Danny's stretcher.

She did a quick assessment of Mike. He smelled of smoke. His eyes were red. The suspenders of his bunker pants hung at his legs. His left arm was in a sling. There didn't seem to be any deformities. Had he really popped his shoulder back in? She winced at the thought.

"See something there?" Danny asked, mistaking her

expression for concern that he might have suffered some burns or bruising.

"You're fine," Dr. Frank said. "Let's get you off this board. We'll roll him on three."

Alex held onto Danny while Mike, using his good arm, helped pull the board out from under the big man.

"Don't sit up too fast," Alex warned.

"I'm fine. Stop all the fuss." Danny dangled his feet off the side of the stretcher.

"We need one more sample." Dr. Frank handed Danny a specimen cup. "I'll send someone in with a wheelchair."

"Wheelchair?" Danny responded in horror. With Mike close by for support, he made a vain attempt to rise. Still unsteady on his feet he sat back down and waited for a wheelchair.

An aide arrived to assist Danny to the bathroom. "You two wait here for me," Danny ordered.

"I've got labs to check," Dr. Frank said. He pulled the curtain around Alex and Mike.

"Are you all as stubborn as Danny?" Alex knew the answer. Mike would be just as independent as his buddy if he were on the other end. "Your arm, is it okay?" She noticed he had slipped his hand out of the sling. She made no attempt to hide the fact that she was assessing him.

"Fine. I've dislocated this shoulder before. I'm getting good at banging it back in by myself." He walked around the stretcher.

Standing close to him gave her comfort. He seemed

to be okay. Soot had darkened his skin but in his blood-shot eyes she noticed a heartrending tenderness.

"You are the best thing I've seen all day." His fingers traced a line down her arms as if he needed to touch her for reassurance that she was real.

"Your shoulder." She didn't pull away. "Shouldn't you put it back in the sling?"

"The doctor recommended rest. Wear the sling as needed, and don't do anything heroic for awhile."

"Did they find something else wrong?" She couldn't hide the worry in her voice. "Did they test your oxyhemoglobin?" She couldn't miss the smoky smell as he pressed her closer.

"The lab results came back fine. I wore my inhaler the whole time, no evidence of smoke inhalation. My X-ray showed almost normal placement of my shoulder." He held her at arms length, showing her his shoulder moved without difficulty.

"You'll need to rest; be out on benefits?"

"As long as I need. Don't worry."

"I'll have to ask my grandfather and Chloe to keep you busy in the shop so you won't get bored."

"I don't plan on getting bored." He smiled that sly, suggestive smile that made her heart skip a beat. "Everything else is working fine." He pulled her close.

She put her hands on his chest and felt the strong beat of his heart.

"What's your diagnosis, nurse?"

"Mike, there's something I have to say." She held up her hand. Now that she had his attention, she wanted to tell him everything that crossed her mind this morning. "I was wrong to react like I did about your bet with the guys."

"No, I'm the one who should be sorry for allowing it to go as far as it did." He reached for both of her hands. "Maybe we could start over without any of that cosmic hocus-pocus."

"I have no idea what today's horoscope predicts." She looked directly in his eyes and added, "And I don't really care. You're safe and that's the best forecast I could ask for."

"And all that nonsense about not dating firemen?"

It was her turn to smile slyly. "I just never met the right firefighter."

"And how do you feel about changing your name to Alex Simone?"

A lump stuck in her throat. She didn't know if she could speak.

"If you want time to think about it, I understand." Mike gripped her hands tighter. "Alex, marry me."

"I don't need to think about it. Of course, I'll marry you." Mike pulled her toward him, his arms encircling her.

"Careful with that shoulder." She put her arms around his neck and smiled. "We've got a wedding to plan."

Mike responded with a shiver of kisses that sealed their destiny.